Three
Indian
Princesses

Also by Jamila Gavin:

✦ ✦

The Whistling Monster:
Stories from Around the World

Danger by Moonlight

Three Indian Goddesses:
The stories of Kali, Lakshmi and Durga

Three Indian Princesses

WALKER
BOOKS

To my parents,
who gave me the best of two worlds
J.G.

First published in Great Britain 1987

This edition published 2011 by Walker Books Ltd
87 Vauxhall Walk, London SE11 5HJ

2 4 6 8 10 9 7 5 3 1

Text © 1987 Jamila Gavin
Illustrations © 2011 Uma Krishnaswamy

This book has been typeset in Cochin

Printed and bound in Great Britain by Clays Ltd, St Ives plc

British Library Cataloguing in Publication Data:
a catalogue record for this book is available
from the British Library

ISBN 978-1-4063-3096-0

www.walker.co.uk

CONTENTS

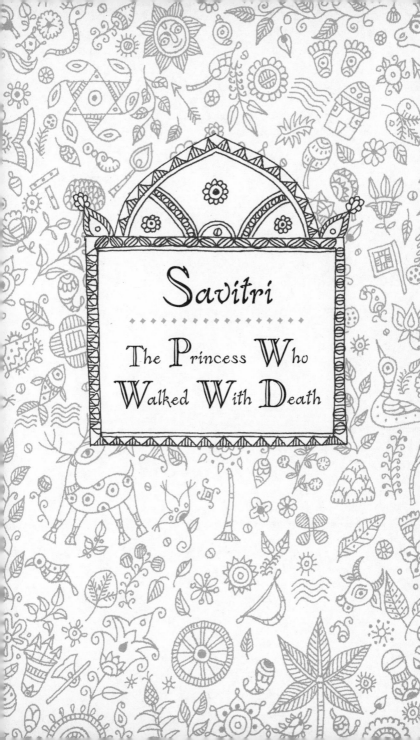

Savitri

• • • • • • • • • • • • • •

The Princess Who Walked With Death

CHAPTER ONE
Into the Jungle

SAVITRI WAS A BEAUTIFUL PRINCESS who lived in India hundreds of years ago. Her eyes were like lotus flowers. Her skin was the colour of sunbeams. Her hair was shining and long and as black as night. Savitri was a very rich princess. Her sarees were made of the very finest silks, and she was always covered in jewels.

Her home was a magnificent palace with large beautiful rooms to explore, and cool courtyards with fountains in which to rest. And all around were the palace gardens with their intricate flower-beds, avenues of cypress trees and shady paths among the guava groves. But over the walls where the sun always set, where the rest of the world spread away to the shimmering horizon; over the wall was the jungle.

Savitri could see the jungle from her balcony. She could hear the jungle from her bed. Each morning she loved to watch the green parrots burst upwards from the treetops into the pink, dawn sky and swoop round the palace. She loved to catch a glimpse of the spotted deer as they sprang through the dappled shadows; or the grey mongoose spinning and curling down the old, gnarled trunks of the trees. Sometimes she saw a small solemn boy herding dusty buffalo down to the river. Sometimes she saw the village children running almost naked through the long grass only to disappear laughing and squealing into the jungle. How she longed to throw off her fine clothes and join them. How she longed to fling off her leather sandals and feel more than the hard, white marble beneath her feet.

One afternoon when her old ayah was dozing in the heat of the day, the gardener was bent intently over his rose bushes and her chosen playmates were quarrelling on the swing, Savitri slipped away. From her balcony, she had often noticed a small door in the palace walls. Savitri was determined now to find this door. Hoisting up her saree, she ran through the palace gardens until she reached the high, grey boundary walls. Then trailing her fingers along its ancient stones, she walked and walked for several minutes.

Suddenly, there it was. Just a small, wooden door. The only thing that stood between her and the outside world. She pushed it and it opened. For a few moments Savitri stood absolutely still, just gazing in wonder. There was the jungle not more than three paces away, green and dense and very, very wild.

Savitri stepped outside. A little path ran before her and twisted away out of sight among the thick, hanging creepers and the long grass. It seemed to beckon her to follow. She thought, "I'll just walk a little way along, just a little way to see what it's like in the jungle."

She moved forwards cautiously, feeling the hot sun burning into her back. Then she quickened her pace and with one more step she stood within the dark shade of the jungle. A wonderful coolness descended upon her. It was the coolness and peace of the temple, and she felt no fear. She began to walk further and further, as if an invisible thread drew her deeper into the forest. And oh, the sights which entranced her eyes! Inquisitive, long-tailed monkeys hung upside down gazing at her, mocking and chattering; a peacock trailed its glittering feathers of purple and gold across her path; the wild elephant paused for a moment to study her, then tossed its trunk upwards and continued to tear the juicy leaves from the overhanging branches.

Suddenly there was a rustle in the undergrowth. The monkeys screeched and swung upwards into the treetops; a large bird rose squawking from the bushes and flapped noisily away. Savitri froze, her breath held, her heart hardly daring to beat. The jungle was a dangerous place. How often had her ayah told her that? How often had she heard stories of deadly snakes that coiled in the hollows; of poisonous spiders, and insects with stings of fire? And most terrifying of all, how often had she listened, her arms clasped around her knees, her back prickling with fright, to stories about the tiger? Yes, she had forgotten about the tiger when she stepped through that little door. She had forgotten about the Lord of the Jungle. This cunning beast of black and gold, so secretive and deadly that he brought terror wherever he stalked.

Savitri wanted to run, but her legs wouldn't move. She wanted to scream, but her voice was paralysed. She felt she was dead already, when suddenly something struck her hard on her head. She was so surprised that she cried out. Then she was struck on the shoulder and then her ankle. She whirled round hopping with pain. She heard a muffled laugh somewhere above her head. Her fear turned to anger.

"Who dares to strike me?" she demanded in her princess's voice. "I'll have you whipped!" There was another laugh and an acorn flew through the air and landed at her feet. She looked up and caught a glimpse of a boy's mischievous face grinning at her through the branches. One hand was raised ready to throw another acorn at her.

"Don't you dare!" she screamed. "I'll call the palace guards!"

The cheeky smile immediately disappeared from the boy's face. He withdrew behind a thick cluster of foliage and with barely a sound was gone. All was silent. Savitri was sorry she had been so angry. She called out. "Come back! Please come back! I didn't mean it!"

Still there was silence. Savitri sighed with disappointment and turned to go home when another acorn rolled gently before her. The boy had come back.

He stood at a safe distance regarding her. He looked very poor. He had no sandals on his feet, and not even a cotton shirt on his back. All he wore was a rough reddish garment made from the bark of trees. It was the sort of garment holy men wear when they give up everything to live at peace with God in the jungle.

"Who are you?" asked Savitri, not in her princess's voice.

"I am Prince Satyvan," replied the boy simply.

Savitri burst out laughing. "You, a prince? What a silly game to play! I know what princes look like. They wear silk shirts and golden sandals and long, flowing turbans covered in jewels. I've never seen a prince look like you!"

"My father, the king, became blind. My wicked uncle drove him out of his kingdom without anything. My mother and I fled with him to live with the hermits in the jungle," explained the boy. Then he pressed the palms of his hands together and bowed politely. "You must be Princess Savitri," he said. "What are you doing here, alone in the jungle?"

"I was bored," cried Savitri. "Bored with the palace, bored with the gardens and bored with my friends who do nothing but quarrel. I've always wanted to see what the jungle was like."

"I have to collect herbs and spices for our evening meal. Will you help me?" asked Satyvan with a friendly smile.

Savitri was delighted. "You'll have to show me which leaves to pick. I've never done anything like this before!"

The two children wandered side by side through the jungle. Satyvan showed her all the different leaves and berries which were safe to eat or use for cooking. He would pluck a leaf and crush it between his fingers. "Smell it!" he cried, as a fragrant aroma rose into the air. Soon Savitri's fingers were smelling of lemon mint, and coriander and wild garlic. She took off her delicate silk veil in which to lay the sprigs of herbs, and when at last they had collected enough, she folded her veil and tied it into a bundle.

They approached a small clearing in the forest. A smell of wood smoke drifted through the trees. "Now I will show you my royal palace," announced Satyvan. Savitri looked round in confusion. She could see no walls of a palace, no dwelling of any sort. All she could see was an old woman dressed in the same red bark as Satyvan, kneeling before a fire fanning the embers with a large leaf. "The old woman is guarding the sacred flame while my mother and father and all the others have gone to search for food and fetch water from the river," explained Satyvan. Then he led Savitri towards a great tree, so ancient and wild that its roots twisted up above the earth, and arched before plunging back into the ground again.

Satyvan dropped down on his knees and crawled beneath the roots into a deep hollow right in the very middle of the tree. "This is my home," he said. Savitri, who had crawled in behind him, gasped with amazement. She could not believe that anyone could live so simply. In one corner were three round brass cooking pots; in another corner were three rolled bed mats made from cane and tiger grass; and in the smallest corner, raised on a little shelf among the roots was one, simple shrine. It was a statue of the God, Vishnu, garlanded with wild flowers.

"Is that all?" breathed Savitri.

"Of course not!" shouted Satyvan. "Here is the rest of my palace!" He dragged her out of the hollow and ran into the middle of the clearing. "See! How high are the ceilings of my palace," he cried, throwing up his arms towards the sky. "And how rich are my walls!" He pointed to the great trees of the forest bursting with flowers and fruit. "Do you not think this is the greatest, richest palace you have ever seen?"

Savitri gazed in awe at the jungle around her and knew that it was true.

Suddenly Satyvan saw how low the sun had sunk, and how the shadows of the trees now stretched like bars across the ground. "You must go home. It's getting late," he said anxiously. He took her hand and led her back along the path until they were once more in sight of the palace walls.

Before Savitri slipped back through the little door in the wall, she said, "Thank you, Satyvan. Thank you for showing me your palace." Then they waved goodbye, promising they should meet again.

CHAPTER TWO
Savitri Makes Her Choice

THE PALACE WAS IN AN UPROAR. Savitri's absence had soon been discovered, and people had been searching every inch of the palace gardens. Her ayah sat rocking and wailing, her head covered in shame. The gardener wept, as he told the king and queen that one moment she had been there in the garden, and the next moment gone. Her playmates, one by one, told of when they had last seen her. They searched in all her favourite hiding places. They shouted and called and blamed each other.

Into all this panic and confusion stepped Savitri. Everyone gasped in astonishment. Her hair had untwisted from its neat coil and hung in long straggles round her shoulders; her silk veil was gone; she carried her sandals in her hand; and her beautiful rich clothes were torn and dusty and tangled with leaves. She looked at them all, her face smudged with earth and bark, her fingers stained with plucking herbs and berries. "I'm sorry if you've been worried about me," she whispered. "I only wanted to see the jungle."

Her mother burst into tears and clasped her daughter in her arms. Her servants and ayah fell howling at her feet and kissed them and touched her to make sure she was alive. Her playmates rushed around her squealing and crying, "We've been driven mad looking for you!"

Then her father, the king, solemn and unsmiling, summoned her to his chamber. With her head bowed, trembling and ashamed, she stood before him. Only now did she realize what she had done. "I only wanted to see the jungle," she wept. "I only wanted to run free like the children outside the palace. Please forgive me."

A long time passed before Savitri emerged from her father's chamber. She looked pale and tired, but she was smiling. First her father had listened to her story; then he had scolded her for putting herself into such danger, and causing so much worry. Finally he had taken her on his knee and hugged her with joy. Savitri was his only child and he loved her more than all the world.

Then her mother, her ayah and handmaidens led Savitri away to her chamber. They bathed her in soft rose-scented water, and scrubbed away all the dust and smells of the jungle. They oiled and massaged her body till her skin glistened like honey. Her long, tangled hair was washed and combed and plucked free of twigs and leaves, and then warm coconut oil was rubbed into her scalp and worked through her black tresses.

When at last she was as clean and sweet-smelling as a princess should be, they slipped her into a delicate, silk nightdress and laid her in her soft feathered bed.

But Savitri couldn't sleep. She lay watching the strange, flickering shadows on her ceiling thrown by the oil lamp which was her night light. She listened to the low sounds of the jungle, that vast kingdom out there beyond the palace walls. She wondered if Satyvan was lying on his bedroll of leaves in the middle of the tree, listening to the same sounds.

Suddenly, a low growl made her sit upright, tense with excitement. "Ayah! Did you hear that?" she whispered. But her ayah, exhausted with the events of the day, lay curled up at the foot of her bed sound asleep.

Trying not to rustle her sheets, Savitri slid from her bed and went out onto her balcony overlooking the jungle. At first the darkness was like a black wall. The moon was a fine sickle above her head, and gave no light as Savitri strained her eyes trying to see beyond the palace walls. Then two green eyes burned like flames of fire. They seemed to be staring straight up at her. A huge shape separated itself from the blacker depths of the jungle and moved towards the palace. Savitri shuddered with fear and wonderment. The eyes held her for a moment and then turned and vanished. Savitri sighed with contentment. Now she felt her day was truly over, and she went back to bed and slept till the sun was high in the noon sky.

The next day the king's wise sage and counsellor came to his side. "Your Highness," he said, "I have consulted my ancient books, and studied the position of all the stars and the planets. I have examined the princess's horoscope in detail, and all the signs say that the time has come for your daughter to be married. Perhaps then she will no longer be gripped by such wildness."

The king listened thoughtfully. "If it is so written in the ancient books, and if the stars and planets are favourable, then I will order it," he said at last. But his heart was sad and heavy. He loved his daughter more than life itself, and could not bear to think that one day she must marry and leave his palace.

When Savitri heard that she must prepare to be married, her heart too became heavy with sorrow. But she smiled at her father to hide her pain, and answered simply that she would do his bidding. "I ask only one thing," she said. "That I be allowed the husband of my choice."

The king willingly agreed, and soon messengers were sent galloping throughout the kingdom and far beyond. They carried the news across the desert plains to the mountain kingdoms of the great Himalayas; they crossed mighty rivers to deliver the news to the great red-stoned cities of the East, and the holy cities of the West; and they followed the seashore southwards until they reached the palm-tossed kingdom on the Indian Ocean.

Soon princes began to arrive at the palace. Princes of every shape and size came hurrying to offer themselves, for Savitri's beauty and goodness were famous throughout that part of the world.

There were fat princes, lying perspiring among their jewelled cushions, carried in swaying sedans by panting servants. There were pompous princes who arrived sitting like gods on the tops of great, decorated elephants. Some came like warriors, galloping in on magnificent horses, brandishing bronze shields and glittering spears. Others arrived like exotic travellers, tossing proudly on the backs of arrogant camels. All came with precious gifts such as no princess had ever seen in her life before.

Savitri sat between her mother and father and graciously received them all. As each one presented himself, the king's sage and counsellors consulted their books. They examined and compared the horoscopes, studied the stars and interpreted the omens.

Sometimes they shook their heads, and an unlucky prince would depart in sorrow, for no one who gazed upon Savitri failed to fall in love with her. Other times they would raise their hands as a signal that the omens were good and the stars favourable. Then a hopeful prince would stand joyfully to one side to await the princess's decision. It took nearly a year before all the princes had been seen, and either selected to await a decision, or sent home disappointed.

At last the king took his daughter's hand and led her to a secret window. From here she could gaze down into a courtyard below. "There you see six of the finest princes in the land," said the king. "Each prince is not only handsome and wealthy, but above all, noble in action, word and deed. Choose one of these, and I know you'll be happy."

Princess Savitri studied each prince for a long time, but finally said, "I'm sorry, Father. Although I see before me princes who are handsome and worthy, and in whose faces goodness shines so bright, yet I do not see a prince who I could love."

"But my daughter!" exclaimed the king. "You have seen every prince there is to be seen from all the farthest corners of India. The princes you see before you are the flower of royal princes. There are no others worthy to be brought before you."

"There is one prince who has not been brought before me," said Savitri.

The king was amazed. "Who can that be?" he asked.

"Prince Satyvan," replied Savitri quietly. "His kingdom is just a short distance from here."

The king sent for his sage and all his counsellors

and demanded to know why Prince Satyvan had not been invited to see the princess.

"Prince Satyvan!" cried one advisor. "But he has no kingdom any more!"

"He lives in poverty in the jungle!" cried another. "We couldn't ask him!"

"Prince Satyvan was thrown out of his kingdom along with his blind father, the king, and his mother. They live with the hermits in the forest," explained the sage. "But though I have heard say that this prince is of exceptional holiness and has all the virtues of a saint; that he is as brave as the bravest warrior, and possessed of all the worthiest qualities, yet he has no wealth and no kingdom. He could not possibly be a suitable husband for your daughter."

"Well then, that's settled," agreed the king. "Come, Savitri! Choose one of these six fine princes, and let the wedding celebrations commence!"

Savitri solemnly turned her lotus eyes on her father's face. "You promised me that I could have the husband of my choice. Well then, I choose Satyvan."

The king and all his advisors were astonished and bewildered. "But why?" they asked, shaking their puzzled heads. "How can a princess like you choose a pauper who has nothing but the jungle for a kingdom?"

"Is it not written in the ancient, holy books that only once can a maid choose a husband?" asked Savitri. "Well, I have chosen. My choice is Satyvan and I will make no other choice."

The king's sage took his ancient books and retired to a corner to see what the stars and planets had to say on the matter. He sat for many hours, his head bent low over the yellow pages, tugging his white beard as he made his calculations. At last he looked up, blinking his tired eyes and straightening his aching back. "It is true that Satyvan is as noble and pure as any prince in the universe. He is possessed of so many virtues and such goodness of heart that he is worthy to be counted among the gods!"

"You see!" cried Savitri, clapping her hands with joy. "Now don't you think he's worthy enough to be my husband?"

"Wait," commanded the sage gravely. "I must still advise you that this marriage cannot take place."

"Why?" gasped Savitri, flushing with distress. "What else have you found to stand in my way?"

"It is also written in the stars that Prince Satyvan will die in exactly one year from now."

The colour drained from Savitri's face. Her blood ran cold and she stood like one frozen. The king came up to her gently and held her icy hand. "I'm sorry, my child," he said with tears of pity. "Come now, forget Satyvan and choose one of these fine young men."

But Savitri would only repeat, "It is written that only once can a maid choose a husband. I have made my choice. Even if he had only one day to live I would not make any other choice. I will marry Satyvan."

The king and the old sage looked at each other. "I will not stand in her way any longer," said the counsellor.

The king embraced his daughter and said, "Then let it be so. Tomorrow we will go into the forest and ask the blind king's permission for you to marry Satyvan."

CHAPTER THREE
One Year to Live

THE NEXT MORNING a magnificent procession gathered in the main marble courtyard. It was a glittering sight of shiny prancing horses on which were seated the royal soldiers in scarlet uniforms, carrying bronze spears and shields. Camels looked down their proud noses as wonderful baskets of gifts were strapped to their backs by servants in brilliant white uniforms with silken sashes and turbans of orange and green. Musicians and dancing girls whirled about, beating drums and clashing cymbals. In the middle of it all stood a vast, royal elephant. How magnificent he looked painted from head to tail with intricate patterns of beautiful colours: and firmly fixed on his back was the royal howdah of scarlet, with gold curtains and cushions, for the king and his daughter to sit in.

The king led Savitri out of the palace, and the huge elephant gracefully lowered his great body and knelt at their feet. A servant ran forward to assist the princess up onto the elephant's back, but Savitri suddenly stopped.

"Father," she said to the king. "Do you think it is right to approach a poor, blind king with all this pomp and ceremony? What does he wish to know of all our wealth and finery? He cannot see, and it will not prove that I am worthy to marry his son. Please let us walk alone, you and I, into the forest. I will take you along the path I found a year ago. Let us find the blind king together and ask his permission."

The king looked down with awe on his young daughter. She had changed over the last twelve months from being a wild, carefree child into a young woman of noble purpose and calm strength, and he knew she was right. He waved his hand and dismissed the procession.

Joyfully, Savitri took her father's hand and led him through the palace gardens to the little wooden door in the wall. Once more she pushed it open and they both stepped out on to the threshold of the jungle.

The king and the princess followed the path through the forest. They marvelled together at the glorious flowers which festooned their way, and the fine-feathered birds that strutted across their path. She sometimes ran into the undergrowth to show her father some of the herbs and spices Satyvan had taught her to recognize for cooking, and they picked juicy, wild fruit to quench their thirst.

At last they reached the small clearing in the forest. There was Satyvan, on his knees tending the sacred flame.

"Prince Satyvan!" The king called his name. "I have come to ask for an audience with your father, the king. I wish to ask his consent for you to marry my daughter."

Satyvan stood up slowly, amazed by what he heard. It seemed impossible. Then he looked at Savitri's face and saw all her love for him shining there.

He ran to the great tree which was his home and disappeared inside among the roots to find his father. After a while Satyvan emerged from the hollow. He stooped to help the blind king who crawled out behind him. Although both father and son stood bare-footed, wearing nothing but their covering of red bark, and looking as poor as the poorest in the land, yet they stood side by side with regal dignity, waiting to receive their guests as though they were in the most royal of palaces.

"Your Highness!" exclaimed Savitri's father, stepping forward. "I have a daughter who is known far and wide for her beauty and excellence. She could have picked a husband from among the hundreds of warrior princes and wealthy kings of this land. Yet she has told me that there is only one man on this earth that she wishes to marry and that is your son, Satyvan."

"How can this be?" cried the blind king tremulously. "Look at us. We live a life of great poverty and hardship. From morning until dusk we do nothing but work and pray. There is no luxury here but the sound of birdsong, and fragrant smells of flowers and herbs. Her palace would be a tree, and her bed the hard earth. How could a gentle princess endure all this?"

"My daughter knows that true happiness cannot be found through wealth and luxury. She knows that she would have to endure a far greater poverty without the husband that she loves. The deprivation of the soul is far greater than the deprivation of the body. She says that only once can a maid choose a husband, and she has chosen Satyvan."

The blind king took Savitri's hands. He felt her soft, sensitive fingers which had never known work. He touched her delicate cheeks which had never known the heat of the day or the chill of winter nights. He ran his fingers over her clear brow and felt the lines of her mouth and the determination of her chin.

"My child," he whispered, "is this what you truly wish? This poor, young man for a husband, and a helpless, blind hermit for a father?"

"That is what I wish," replied Savitri.

So Savitri and Satyvan were married. It was a simple ceremony held in the forest round the sacred flame. Savitri came with no dowry. She brought with her only the goodness of her heart and her deep love for Satyvan. She gave up all her fine clothes and jewellery; she gave up her many handmaidens and faithful ayah. She put on the rough, red garment of the hermits, and set about learning to live the harsh, austere life of the forest dwellers.

But to Savitri it was no hardship. At last she was in the jungle. She took to her new life eagerly and joyfully.

She learned how to make the fire and keep it kindled. She learned how to chop wood and fetch water from the stream. She gathered herbs and fruit, and learned to grind the spices and prepare the meal. Everything that she did, she did with such happiness, that no one guessed the terrible secret she kept deep, deep down inside herself; the terrible knowledge that every day that passed was a day closer to Satyvan's death.

The weeks and months fled by. It was as if the world was being spun by a team of galloping horses, faster and faster, and there was nothing Savitri could do to slow down the pace. But still not one flicker of anguish showed on her face and she continued to love her husband with all her heart, and to look after his parents with every devotion. Time slipped away until there were only seven days left. Seven days before Satyvan must die.

Telling Satyvan and his parents that she must have a few days alone in the forest to pray and meditate, Savitri found a solitary place. She built herself a small shelter with leaves and branches and crawled inside. Here she sat cross-legged for six days and nights without moving to eat or drink or even sleep. She emptied her mind of all thought and her body of all feeling. With her eyes closed she concentrated her energies into a blue light which seared through her like a flame. It was as if her whole body was cleansed so that she could communicate with the gods. For six days and nights she sat in this trance while the sun rose and set, and the moon dwindled and paled into a silver stroke of light in the sky. All around her the jungle heaved in its struggles with life and death; the cheetah stalked the deer; snakes arched and poised, their tongues flickering, ready to strike; the herons swooped along the river banks while frogs froze in the reeds. And the tiger who was Lord of the Jungle paced his deadly way through the night, seeking man or beast to drag back to his den.

But Savitri sat in perfect stillness until the seventh day. Just before the grey light of dawn glimmered on the horizon, she came out of her trance. Getting slowly to her feet she stretched, then walked down to the river to bathe before walking back through the dewy forest to her husband.

CHAPTER FOUR
Encounter With Death

SATYVAN GREETED HER WITH JOY and wonderment. She was so pale and thin that her body looked transparent in the early morning light. Yet her face glowed with a powerful radiancy as she called out to him. "Ah, Satyvan, have I come just in time to accompany you into the forest?"

Satyvan begged her to stay and rest. "I'll go and find you the choicest fruits and herbs. I'll prepare you the finest of meals to restore your strength."

"You are my strength," cried Savitri. "By your side I could walk to the ends of the earth. Do not ask me to stay behind, not today of all days." She took his hand.

"Have you ever known such a beautiful day as today?" she asked.

There did indeed seem to be something special about this day. Satyvan felt it as he gazed around him. They say that the cycle of the universe is but the breathing in and the breathing out of Brahma himself; ten thousand years to breathe in and ten thousand years to breathe out. Today it was as if Brahma paused for a moment as he breathed in, held his breath – just for an instant – as he too marvelled at the wondrous world he had created. The colours of the jungle seemed sharper and more dazzling; the trills and whistles and gruntings and chatterings of the birds and beasts sounded united in a chorus of praise and ecstasy; the myriad layers of smells and perfumes that rose from the earth and wafted from the trees and flowers flooded through his nostrils and intoxicated him. Satyvan had never felt more alive. All his senses were tingling with the impact of life. As the sun poured its golden rays through the leafy treetops, he felt as if somehow he and Savitri were being blessed by the gods.

"You are right," he whispered. "Today we must be together." Encircling an arm round her waist to support her, Satyvan gently led Savitri down the forest track.

The forest itself seemed to lean towards the couple. Juicy fruit hung from the branches just within reach; bushes laden with herbs and spices spilled across their path; the deer, usually so shy, paused in the undergrowth and watched them pass; a peacock stretched his purple neck and fanned out his fantastic tail of green, purple and golden eyes.

At last they reached a small, leafy clearing. The sun, now at its zenith, had brought a hush to the forest as everything rested in the searing heat. Savitri found a spreading bower and lay down to rest in its shade. Only Satyvan seemed untroubled by the heat. He swung his axe in great swoops and whistled and sang as he chopped down a tree for firewood. Savitri watched him through half shut eyes. She felt lulled into peacefulness, yet never willing to take her eyes off him for a single moment.

Suddenly Satyvan gave a sharp cry. His axe froze above his head, then dropped from his hands. Savitri sat up with a moan of anguish, and rushed forward to catch him as his body fell headlong to the ground.

"Savitri!" he groaned. "My head is burning, yet such a terrible chill runs through my body."

Savitri knelt over him so that her body cast a shade over his head. She squeezed the juice of a mango between his lips, and massaged his limbs to ease the aching. And all the while, she prayed and prayed, and begged the gods not to take Satyvan from her. But though she pressed her mouth to his and tried to breathe her own life into his body, she felt him shudder beneath her, and saw the light fading from his eyes.

Now, though the sun was still a blazing orb above their heads, the sky began to darken all around them, and it became like night. The forest itself seemed to be lost in an ocean of darkness. Savitri lay on the ground, her arms clasped round Satyvan as she tried to hold the last gasps of life inside him. Approaching through this terrible void glowed a pair of eyes. They were not the glowering green eyes of the tiger. These eyes burned red like the hottest coals in the middle of a fiery furnace. Nearer they came and nearer, until they halted over the young couple on the ground.

Slowly Savitri raised her eyes and gazed into those burning sockets.

A great black figure stood over her in a hooded swirling cloak. In his hands he held a noose which hung directly over Satyvan's heart. Like a low, throbbing chord, a voice spoke. "Do you know who I am?"

Savitri answered fearlessly. "Yes, I know who you are. You are Lord Yama, Lord of the Dead."

"I have come to take Satyvan's soul to paradise," said Lord Yama, slowly dropping his noose lower and lower.

"My Lord!" cried Savitri. "Why have you come in person? I thought a messenger of death was always sent."

"I know that Satyvan has led a perfect and blameless life, and I know that you, as his wife, have tried to achieve perfection in the eyes of the gods. Your efforts have not gone unnoticed. Your prayers and fastings have impressed me so much that I wanted to come in person to show you my pleasure, and to be the one to take Satyvan's soul straight to paradise." Then Lord Yama dropped the noose so low that it touched Satyvan's chest. At that moment Satyvan's soul leaped from his body as all his limbs gave one last quivering shudder. Yama's noose pulled tight and caught the soul, still struggling, and quickly bound it securely. "Be comforted, fair Savitri," said Lord Yama. "When your time comes you will join your husband in paradise." Then he turned towards the south and sped swiftly away.

Choking with grief Savitri knelt by her husband's body as the swirling darkness ebbed away. She kissed the cold face she had loved so well, and tried to find some glimmer of him in his open unseeing eyes. But dust was already beginning to settle on his lifeless body, and she realized that Satyvan was gone. She realized that everything that was Satyvan was bound up in Lord Yama's noose.

She leaped to her feet and gazed southwards. She could just see the last ripples of darkness surrounding Yama as he dwindled into the distance.

Savitri ran. Desperation gave her speed. Her love for Satyvan made her unafraid. She ran and ran until at last she caught up with the God of Death.

Lord Yama stopped and turned. It was as if a volcano burned inside his head; as if molten lava swam in his eyes as he gazed upon her sternly. "Savitri! Why do you follow? Return immediately!"

"I must follow," replied Savitri. "You have my husband, and wherever he goes, I go."

"You have proved yourself to be a loyal and devoted

wife, but now your duties are over. Go back and comfort those who are in mourning and prepare the burial rites," commanded the god. "And because I admire you, Savitri, and appreciate your goodness, I will grant you one wish. Only don't ask for Satyvan's life. That wish I will never grant."

"My Lord," murmured Savitri gratefully. "I do have a wish, and that is to have the gift of sight returned to my blind father-in-law."

"Your wish is granted," said Lord Yama, speeding on his way again. "Return now, Savitri! Follow me no more."

But Savitri did not turn back. Instead she broke into a run to keep pace with the god's long stride.

"Go back, Savitri! Do not disobey me. It is forbidden to walk and talk with the gods," cried Yama, increasing his speed.

"Forgive me for reminding you," panted Savitri, "but the rules of hospitality say that if two people walk more than seven paces together, they become companions, and must converse politely together. I have walked more than seven paces with you, so I am your companion now and have a right to talk to you."

Yama slowed down so that Savitri could stop running to keep up. "Why do you not return to the forest? Your husband's body is lying there. It could be attacked by wild animals. Go and see that it is properly prepared for the funeral and I will grant you another wish. Ask anything – except for Satyvan's life."

"I do have a wish," said Savitri. "I wish that my father-in-law could have his kingdom returned to him so that he may once more rule justly and wisely as he did before."

"Your wish is granted," cried Lord Yama. "Now go back."

Savitri looked around her and shuddered. They had now entered a steep, grey, stony valley. Great sheets of rock sheered upwards on either side, so high that even the sun's blazing rays were barred from entering. Their jagged peaks cut the chill sky like razors, and not even vultures circled above to show any sign of life in that dreadful place. When she spoke, her voice broke up into a million reverberating echoes.

"My Lord!" trembled Savitri, clutching her arms around her for warmth. "When I made my marriage vows I swore that I would follow my husband wherever he went, so that is why I am still at your side. Besides, it is truly wonderful to be in the presence of a god as magnificent and gracious as you are."

"Fair Savitri," said Lord Yama. "Your words are pleasing to my ears, and I admire your faithful devotion. But Satyvan is dead and your vows have no more meaning. You are no longer a wife, but you are still a daughter. So go now and comfort Satyvan's parents who must be grieving and alone, and I will grant you another wish – except of course I cannot grant you Satyvan's life."

"If my father-in-law has both his sight and his kingdom, then he will need heirs to carry on after him. Grant, I beseech you, that he may have sons to replace Satyvan."

"It will be so," answered Lord Yama. "Your father-in-law will be blessed with many heirs, and his line will continue for hundreds of years. Now go. Go. This is no land for mortals."

The Lord of Death turned his face southwards again and continued on his way. For an instant Savitri watched the great black god swirl onwards into that bleak valley. Although he was moving further and further away, yet he seemed to be increasing in size until he was towering among the lonely crags. His great, sable cloak billowed out around him as if it contained the whole black universe within it. Terror froze Savitri to the spot, and her courage almost failed her. Then she saw the god's long staff slung across his shoulder, and the small tight bundle on the end of it which contained Satyvan's soul. With a cry that echoed like splintering glass she sprang forward and followed.

As she caught up with Lord Yama she stretched out an anguished hand to tug his sleeve. It was like clutching air, and her fingers touched nothing but darkness.

"Take me too, oh God of Death!" she wept. "I cannot bear to be separated from Satyvan. I know that you have the power over life and death, that you choose who should live and who should die. I have performed all my penances; I have fasted and prayed and done all I can to please the gods. Do not separate us."

When Lord Yama turned, darts of fire leaped from his eyes, but compassion made his face beautiful, and Savitri did not flinch as she stared up at him.

"Oh, Savitri! Savitri!" Lord Yama sighed. "Your

goodness alone makes you worthy enough to step straight into paradise. But it is not time for you yet. You must wait patiently and then I will come myself and collect your soul. Turn back, fair princess. Turn back. You still have duties to perform. You must prepare Satyvan's body for the funeral and you must comfort his parents. I will grant you one more wish, only do not, do not ask for Satyvan's life, or for your death."

"My Lord!" replied Savitri. "I know that of all the gods you are the most powerful in the world of mankind. My wish is that I should have many sons and daughters to comfort and support me through my life."

"So be it, Savitri," declared Lord Yama. "I willingly grant you that wish. Now go!"

As their voices echoed and re-echoed, merging together into incredible harmonies, Savitri suddenly saw the River. This was the river which separated the living from the dead, and the gods from Man. It flowed broad and heavy and deep and dark. Its great, liquid mass swirled and coiled into interlocking whirlpools in which it seemed all the souls of the dead were circling and revolving.

Lord Yama moved steadily and irrevocably towards this river. Without a pause he stepped into its flow. The current caught his cloak and swept it outwards till it was part of the water. The torrent surged round his knees as if he were a rock, for he did not falter. He had almost merged into the watery blackness of the river.

"Lord Yama!" Savitri called out. Her voice no longer reverberated, but dried airlessly as soon as it left her lips. She wondered if he had heard.

"Lord Yama!" she called again. "You granted me a wish, but you cannot fulfil it. You granted my wish for many sons and daughters, but how can this be if you do not return my husband to me?"

Across the surface of the water, burning through that deep everlasting blackness she saw two glowing crimson eyes. She knew that he had heard her. They stared at each other, he from midstream, she on the bank of the river, their eyes meeting across the abyss of Life and Death.

Then the message came to her. Was it his voice which sounded like a lonely shepherd piping? Or was it some strange ethereal voice which sang inside her head and told her? Yama raised his staff as if in farewell, and

Savitri could see by the glow of his eyes that the bundle which had been tied on the end was unwrapped, and the bindings flapping loosely.

Savitri placed both palms of her hands together and bowed her head in reverence and thanks. Then she turned and ran.

CHAPTER FIVE
The Return

As Savitri emerged from the chill, grey valley of death, the full heat of the sun struck her. Shielding her eyes she stared up into the brilliant blue sky and saw that the sun had barely slid a notch from its zenith. She sped back through the forest, back to the small clearing where Satyvan's body lay in the long grass.

She approached him softly and knelt down beside him. She bent and kissed his cold lips. As she did, a quiver ran through his limbs, like a field of corn suddenly quivers when a breeze ruffles through it. She cradled his head in her arms and began to sing quietly.

Many hours passed. The sun dropped lower and lower in the sky and finally sank behind the dense line of forest. Long-fingered shadows crept into the clearing, and all around could be heard the excited chatterings and murmurings of animals.

Satyvan was now breathing steadily as one merely asleep. Suddenly his eyes flew open with a cry of dread. "Savitri!"

"It's all right. I'm here!" She wept joyfully as she held him close.

Satyvan shuddered with fear. "I had a terrible dream. I dreamed Lord Yama came for me and took me to the Land of the Dead. It was only a dream, wasn't it?" He leaped to his feet and looked about him. "It's almost night!" he cried fearfully. "What shall we do? The wild animals will eat us, and who will there be to protect my parents?" He stared desperately like one still in the grip of a nightmare.

"Hush! Hush!" whispered Savitri, putting her arms around him. "You are alive, and you are safe! And see! The moon has risen. There is plenty of light to guide us home. Nothing will harm us. I know that. Come, let us go now, your parents will be worried."

With Satyvan still dazed and shaking with dread, Savitri led her husband through the forest. Though she could hear the distant growls of a prowling leopard, and the sulky howls of a hyena, she was not afraid. The path twisted and dipped through some dense foliage, and for a few seconds the light of the moon was blotted out. Suddenly there before them, a huge shape blocked their path. It was a tiger. Even in the darkness, his black and gold stripes seemed to smoulder with brilliance; his green eyes narrowed to slits as he looked at the helpless couple. His whole body was taut with a deadly strength, waiting to be unleashed on his prey. He could leap like an arrow sprung from a bow and with one blow of his mighty paw smash their skulls. He stared at them long and hard, poised; frozen in thought. Then suddenly he flicked his tail and with one bound disappeared soundlessly into the shadows.

"You see!" whispered Savitri. "The gods are protecting us. Not even the Lord of the Jungle can harm us if the gods don't wish it."

Feeling comforted, Satyvan's strength and courage returned. Instead of leaning helplessly upon his wife, he now stood upright and took her hand. Steadily and fearlessly they walked on through the night towards home.

As they emerged into the clearing where the hermits lived, Satyvan and Savitri saw the blind king and his queen praying before the sacred flame. They had been filled with despair and unable to sleep for fear of what had happened to their children.

Calling softly to them, Satyvan and Savitri rushed forward to embrace them. The blind king turned his face upwards towards his son, tears streaming from his eyes. "Is it really you?" he cried. Then to his amazement and bewilderment, their faces came shimmering into focus. "I can see!" he shouted.

One by one, all Savitri's wishes were granted. A horseman came galloping into the forest to tell the king that his wicked brother was dead, and that the people wanted him back as ruler. Satyvan's father and mother had many sons and daughters to ensure their royal line for hundreds of years. And Savitri? What of this princess who had averted such sorrow and disaster for herself and others?

Although she and Satyvan left the forest to live with the king in his palace and help him to rule his kingdom, they never forgot their love of the jungle. They never forgot the simple hermits with whom they had shared so much poverty and friendship. They often put on the rough, red cloth of the holy ones, and slipped away into the jungle to pray and meditate, and wander in its beauty.

In due course Satyvan became king and Savitri became queen. They ruled in goodness and peace for long, long years, and had many sons and daughters to bring them happiness.

They were well into old age before Lord Yama came silently one night and took them both straight to paradise.

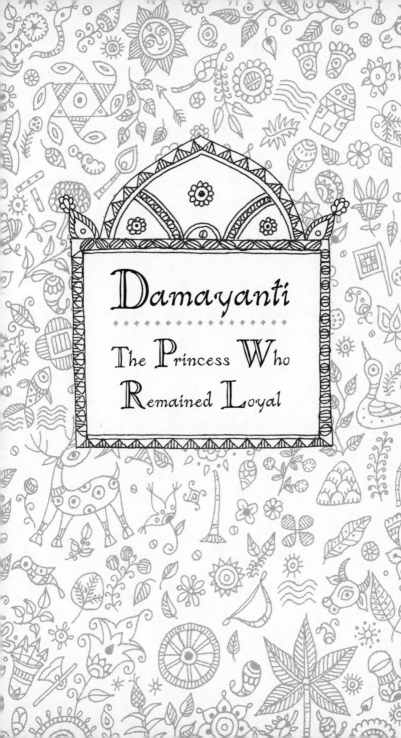

Damayanti

The Princess Who Remained Loyal

CHAPTER ONE
Lord Brahma's Gift

Beneath the ancient branches of a sacred tree King Bhima sat deep in prayer. He had been sitting there since long before dawn, his legs crossed, his arms resting lightly on his knees. As the grey crack of daylight widened in the night sky, a flock of green parrots sprang with a shriek of joy out of the treetops. Their wings beat a tremor through the still air. The king slowly opened his eyes and gazed into the long, tranquil distance. His heart was calm, his mind at peace, even though he carried a deep sorrow inside him.

He and his queen had no children. They were childless after many years of marriage. Who would there be to sit on his throne after he was gone? Worse still, where was the son he would need to light his funeral pyre, and to make sure that his soul was not dragged down to hell? Only a son could do that.

Now with the rising of the sun both man and beast awoke. The low singing of holy songs was heard by the river, and the splashing of water on sleepy bodies as people offered up their morning prayers. King Bhima got to his feet and stretched his arms up to the heavens. He too burst into a hymn of praise and began to stride towards his chambers. Now the crows began their raucous cawing and dogs barked at the palace gates. Servants padded soundlessly to and fro in their bare feet. All through the palace and the city a new day began.

Before the blazing sun had reached its hottest point in the sky, a Brahman came to the palace gates. This man of the priestly caste was called Damana. He had been journeying since dawn, and begged now for a drink of water and a cool spot of shade in which to shelter through the heat of the afternoon. It was King Bhima's rule that no man should be turned away from his gates without hospitality. Even though Damana looked dusty and wild, he was welcomed into the palace and looked after with every courtesy. When evening came, the king insisted that Damana should feed at the royal table and accept a bed for the night so he would be truly rested before setting off the next day.

Damana quietly noted the king's generosity. He noted his kindliness to everyone around him; his justice to the poor of the city; his firmness when dealing with evil. He saw how people laughed and enjoyed themselves in his company, but he also noticed the sadness in his eyes.

Before sunrise the next morning, the Brahman went down to the river to bathe and to say his prayers. Suddenly he realized he was not alone. As he stood waist-deep in the dark swirling waters he heard an anguished sigh. "Brahma! Brahma! Lord of Creation! Hear my prayer and send me a son!" He could just make out the shape of King Bhima praying beneath the sacred tree.

Before Damana stepped out of the river, he took a garland of temple flowers from around his neck. One by one he plucked off the flowers and tossed them into the current. With each flower he sent up a prayer, a prayer that good King Bhima should not be overlooked by the gods.

The white and gold flowers floated away. Their scent wafted upwards. Drifted higher and higher into the heavens until they reached the nostrils of Lord Brahma himself. In the highest, snow-bound peaks of the Himalayas, Lord Brahma sat in his palace and sniffed. As he breathed in the sweet perfume of the temple flowers, he received Damana's prayers and was moved.

"I will reward this rajah, King Bhima," he said with a smile that melted snows. "I will give him and his queen the sons they want, but first, I will send him a special gift of my own. His first child shall be a daughter. Her beauty and goodness shall be equal to goddesses. She shall bear my mark on her forehead as a reminder of the power and generosity of the gods."

The hot season burned and seemed to set everything ablaze. Forest flowers burned orange and gold. The earth burned, too hot for bare feet to touch, too hot even for the snake to slither across. Men and animals hugged the shade silently, too exhausted to speak, waiting for the cool evenings to release their energies. As the end of the season drew near, eyes turned upwards into the burning sky. They strained eagerly, looking for the first signs of the monsoon rain. They prayed to the god, Indra, champion fighter of the Drought Demons, to send the rain.

One day the first cloud was seen. It came lumbering across the sky like a fat, grey elephant. It was followed by another and then another. Low rumbles shook the heavens. As the first plump drops of rain splattered noisily on the cracked earth, a shout of joy arose from the city. King Bhima, seated in prayer under the sacred tree, heard another shout. It overlapped the first, swamping it with its triumphant delight. Yes, the rains had come at last, but so too had a child! King Bhima's queen had given birth as the heavens opened.

King Bhima ran as he had never run before. Shouting with ecstasy, he leaped the fountains, zigzagged through the guava groves and sprang three steps at a time up the palace steps. He reached the queen's chamber panting and gasping for breath. He pushed his way in among the handmaidens. As they bowed before him, did some glance up to see if he minded that his longed-for child was a mere girl?

There was an awed hush as a wizened old woman – the ancient midwife – handed the small bundle to him. "It is a girl, my lord, but see!" the old woman croaked. "She has the mark of Brahma on her brow." Her thin, brown, wrinkled finger pointed to a tiny, lotus-shaped mole just above the baby's left eyebrow.

The king held the child towards the light so that he could see her better. Though just a few moments old, she opened her blue-black eyes and gazed at her father. It was as if all eternity were reflected in them. The whites of her eyes were like the creamy whiteness of the sea of milk at the very beginning of time. Tenderly he handed Brahma's newest creation to his queen.

"We shall call her Damayanti," he said, "after the holy Brahman, Damana, who was our guest and who brought us good fortune by his presence."

"Yes, Damayanti!" sighed the queen, drawing the infant close to her breast.

"Damayanti!" The name was whispered like a gust of wind. It swept out of the bedchamber, through the palace and over the walls into the city. It travelled like wildfire into the bazaars and the market place. On it sped by oxen and horse, by camel and elephant, into the fields and on to the highways, till soon it was repeated in villages and towns right across the kingdom. "King Bhima has a daughter. Her name is Damayanti, and she has the mark of Brahma on her brow!"

CHAPTER TWO
The Swans With the Golden Wings

FROM THE VERY BEGINNING, Princess Damayanti was soul-disturbing. Her beauty trembled like a soft wind ruffling a field of corn, or pale dawn rising from the depths of the ocean. Although she was lavished with gold and rubies and sparkling diamonds, they were only as dewdrops glistening on the petals of a lotus; and though she was surrounded by servants and handmaidens and adoring friends, there was always a certain, quiet loneliness which set her apart.

As she grew older, the palace chatter often turned to who in the world could possibly be a suitable husband for Damayanti.

"There is only one man!" cried a friend.

"Who?" chorused the others, ticking off all the many rajahs and princes in the land.

"Why, King Nala, of course!" came the reply.

"King Nala!" The handmaidens repeated his name, and nodded approvingly. They began to list his qualities.

"He is very rich and powerful."

"He is the finest archer in the land. None can match him."

"He has a stable of the most magnificent horses, and they say he can tame any horse, no matter how wild."

"He is the bravest of warriors, and commands a mighty army."

"They say he is an incarnation of Manu, the first man on earth, and the first law-giver. It's true that he is a just and noble ruler."

"He is pious and god-fearing, too, and reads the Vedas every day."

"And he is very handsome." The handmaidens sighed. Yes, King Nala was a tiger among rajahs, and many a princess would have given up ten kingdoms to be married to him.

"He sounds too perfect," snorted one girl. "He must have some faults."

They all thought for a while, then one cried out. "I know of a fault!"

"What?" they all gasped eagerly.

"He loves playing the dice," she exclaimed.

"Is that all?" They fell back disappointed. "What man doesn't like playing the dice. It only shows he's human, and likes to enjoy life."

"He loves it with a passion," insisted the girl, "and some passions can become weaknesses."

But the others all cried her down, and agreed that Nala's love of dice was more a virtue than a weakness. Nala, they decided, was definitely the only rajah in the world worthy of marrying their precious Princess Damayanti, and they began to tell her about him.

Meanwhile, in the kingdom of Nishadha, King Nala's thoughts had turned to marriage. His friends and counsellors wondered which of the princesses throughout the land were worthy enough to be Nala's queen. But they didn't wonder for too long. There was only one name. There was only one princess they all longed to have as their queen, and that was Damayanti.

King Nala wandered alone among the shady fruit groves of his palace garden. Nowadays, all he could think about was Damayanti. He had never seen her, never met her – yet he had heard so much about her beauty and goodness that already his heart was moved.

Suddenly the air around him was filled with the pounding of wings. A flock of great, white swans came surging down through the sky and landed in the palace lake, tossing up a fountain of spray. They glinted brightly as they stepped out of the water, and as he crept close, Nala saw their wings were flecked with gold.

Stealthily he reached out, and seized the biggest swan round the neck. The bird didn't struggle, although it could have lashed the king with its mighty wings, or pecked his face with its sharp beak. Instead it spoke with a human voice.

"Noble king, do not harm me."

Nala fell back, astonished. "Who are you?" he whispered.

"I am Lord Brahma's favourite bird. I carry the Creator of the Universe on my back when he wishes to travel. I have come to tell you about one of Lord Brahma's most wonderful creations – Princess Damayanti!"

Nala bowed before the swan. "I long for this princess," he murmured. "I have heard she is a pearl among women – like a goddess. How can I hope to win her?"

"Let me go," said the swan with the golden wings, "and I will be your messenger. I will fly to her and tell her things about you so that she will never want to think of any other man."

King Nala was overjoyed. Gladly, he released the swan. His heart was filled with love and hope as he watched the bright flock flap their golden wings, and turn their long white necks towards King Bhima's kingdom.

Princess Damayanti had drifted a little way off from her friends. She was tired of their chattering. These days she felt a restless stirring inside her. All this talk of marriage confused her. She knew the day must come – but her heart ached at the thought of leaving home. She now had three fine and noble brothers, Dama, Danta and Damana – all named after the holy man who had brought her mother and father such joy and good fortune. Could there be any greater happiness outside these palace walls?

Suddenly she heard an excited cry from her companions. A flock of great, white swans came down among them with a rushing of gold wings. Damayanti saw that one swan – the largest of them all – seemed to be waiting for her. It stood tall and white and upright, like a warrior, its golden wings spreading out like brilliant shields.

"Damayanti!" The swan spoke.

The princess gasped.

"I have come to tell you about Nala."

"Everyone sings his praises to me," whispered Damayanti, shyly.

"Of course they do," exclaimed the swan, "for I tell you, there is no man on earth equal to him. You, Damayanti, you with the mark of Brahma on your brow, blessed by the Creator, a pearl among women, if you and he were to marry, then perfect beauty would be married to perfect nobility."

Damayanti trembled as she listened to the strange voice coming from the swan. But the words touched her heart. "Will you speak to Nala as you have spoken to me?" she asked in a small voice.

"Gladly!" cried the swan, and with that, the flock

rose into the air with a whirring of wings, and turned towards Nishadha.

They all gazed up at the sky, watching the gold reflections of the swans' wings merging with the last rays of the sun as it slid below the rim of the earth.

"Tell me more about Nala," begged Damayanti, pulling her friends around her.

CHAPTER THREE
The Swayamvara

LORD INDRA SAT BROODING up in his heaven among the snowy mountain peaks of Mount Meru. Why were so few warriors arriving at his gates these days? A warrior killed in battle usually came to heaven immediately. Where were they? Surely man hadn't given up war? He frowned, and gazed down the snowy mountainside, down to the great Indian plain merging brown and green into the heat haze.

Suddenly he noticed two faint specks moving very, very slowly towards the foot of Mount Meru. Day by day he watched the two specks labouring slowly up the mountain slopes. As they climbed higher and higher, the air got colder, and their breath puffed out in little white coils. Indra waited eagerly. These were two wise men, Narada and Parvata. They had journeyed all the way across India on a pilgrimage to Mount Meru. They would have news and gossip for him.

At last they reached the gates of Indra's palace, and the god hurried to welcome them. When they had bathed, rested and fed, Lord Indra questioned them eagerly.

"What's going on down there on earth? Why are no battle-slain heroes arriving at my gates? What are the rajahs and princes up to?"

"Ah!" sighed the two holy men knowingly. "It's all because of Damayanti."

"Damayanti!" At the sound of that name, the other gods crowded round to listen. There was Agni, Lord of Fire; Varuna, King of the Waters; and Yama, Lord of the Dead. They had all heard of Damayanti, the beautiful daughter of King Bhima.

"Is she really so beautiful?" asked Indra.

"My Lord," nodded the holy men, "she is a pearl among women. She is like a goddess in beauty and goodness. Every king and prince in the land wants to marry her. King Bhima is holding her swayamvara so that she can choose a husband, and every rajah and prince in the land has turned his chariot away from the battlefield, and is galloping to the ceremony. There is only one battle they wish to fight – the battle for her hand."

"Then we must go too!" cried the gods. They leaped into their heavenly chariots and flew through the air towards King Bhima's kingdom.

Also hurrying along the road to the swayamvara was King Nala. Ever since the meeting with the gold-winged swan, his heart was full of joy and expectation. It seemed that he and Damayanti were made for each other – everyone said so! He galloped down the road, his head tossed back, singing loudly.

Looking down from their chariots, the four gods noticed Nala. He looked so handsome – like a god himself – in his silken jacket glittering with jewels, and the upright stately manner in which he sat in the saddle. Even from their height, they could see how noble a king this was, and they said to one another, "Here is the perfect messenger to plead our case with Princess Damayanti." So they floated down through the shimmering air, and landed before the astonished king.

Nala clasped his hands and bowed his head before

the shining beings who stood before him.

"Oh, excellent king!" said Lord Indra. "Mightiest of heroes. We are here on a mission and seek a messenger to do our bidding."

Nala answered in a humble voice. "I see that I am in the presence of celestial beings, and so I willingly agree to serve you in any way I can. May I know who you are, and to whom I must take your message?"

"We are the Four Guardians of the Earth: Indra, Lord of Heaven; Varuna, King of the Waters; Agni, the God of Fire; and Yama, Lord of the Dead. This is our message. Go to Princess Damayanti and tell her that we have heard she seeks a husband. Tell her that we know of her beauty and goodness, that she is as perfect and holy as a goddess. Tell her that we wish her to choose one of us to be her husband."

Nala's fingers whitened as they gripped each other. His heart was filled with a terrible sorrow. "I beg you, my Lords," he pleaded, "find someone else to take your message. I am on my way to the princess's swayamvara, and hope with all my heart to win her hand for myself. How could I put your case to her fairly? Please spare me and send another."

But the gods wouldn't listen. "You made a promise, now you must keep it. Only you are worthy enough to do our bidding. Now go."

Lord Indra waved his hand and in an instant King Nala found himself standing in a cool, sweetly perfumed chamber. There, before him, was the most beautiful girl he had ever seen, and he knew that this was Damayanti. Everything he had been told about her was true. She was more beautiful than the moon. Her eyes were dark, deep pools of magic and her slender body gleamed like a pale willow.

She turned and looked at him with amazement. "Who are you?" Her heart trembled at the sight of this handsome man who had appeared before her like a god.

"I am Nala!" he replied with his heart breaking.

Damayanti gazed at Nala. Everything she had heard about him was true, and she loved him immediately.

"I set off on my journey to your swayamvara as a suitor but now I stand before you as a messenger from the gods." He saw the joy on her face turn to puzzlement. "I have a message for you from the Four Guardians of the Earth: Indra, Agni, Varuna and Yama. News of your beauty and excellence has reached even the mansions of heaven. They feel you are so worthy you must choose one of them as a husband."

Damayanti's eyes filled with tears. "But I have already made my choice," she whispered. "I knew all along that it was you I wanted, and now that I've seen you, I know that I love you."

"You cannot disobey the gods. You will anger them," urged Nala. "Just think, you will be a goddess and live in heaven. Your beauty and youth will never fade."

"But it's you I love," wept Damayanti. "I would suffer anything to know you loved me too."

"If I had not been sent by the Four Guardians of the Earth, I would have spoken for myself," said Nala gently. "So remember me, dear princess."

Damayanti smiled through her tears. "Then I know what we must do. Come to my swayamvara. Enter with the gods, and before them all, I will choose you. They will not be able to hold it against you or me. They know that once a maid chooses, she cannot make a second choice. They will have to abide by my will."

So Nala returned to the Four Guardians of the Earth and told them that Damayanti would make her choice at the swayamvara ceremony. "I have fulfilled my mission, O excellent gods. Now you must await her judgment at the appointed time."

It was the hour of noon, the hour when King Bhima summoned all the suitors to be gathered together in the Great Hall of State. What mighty rajahs passed among the golden pillars, fiercely glittering, proud as lions. Some were powerful-muscled warriors, others oiled and smooth as serpents; what lofty noses and arched eyebrows these great rajahs had, as in their flowing and bejewelled robes they seated themselves on their thrones and waited for Damayanti.

All eyes were on the far entrance, each frozen with expectation. Then suddenly, there was a faint rustle – a swish of silken saree and a jingling of jewellery, and Damayanti appeared in the doorway, dazzling as the sun at midday. She moved down the great hall and all eyes moved with her.

Damayanti looked along the row upon row of royal faces, but there was only one face she wanted to see. Nala! And there he was. Filled with joy, she was just about to run over, toss her garland around his neck and say those eternal words, "I choose you," when she stopped, overcome with confusion. For standing next to him was another Nala, and another and another. Five King Nalas stood before her, all identical. All wore the same clothes, and all looked at her with eyes brimming with love. Then she knew that the Four Guardians of the Earth had tricked her. How could she choose? She studied each face intently. Studied each curve of the lip and slant of the cheek, each bold shoulder with black locks of hair flowing down, and most of all she stared deep into their eyes, looking for some sign to show her the real Nala. But it was no use: each was a mirror image of the next.

Shaking with distress, Damayanti bowed her head and folded her hands in prayer. From within her inmost soul she beseeched the gods to have mercy on her. "Oh, Guardians of the Earth, ever since I was visited by the celestial swan, I pledged myself to Nala. I have never in my life gone back on a pledge for I believe my vow to be holy, and should never be broken. Please help me to keep my promise, and show me Nala."

When the Four Guardians heard her prayer, they were moved, and showed her the signs. The hot noon sun burned down. The heat penetrated the palace. In their flowing robes and jewels, the rajahs began to perspire. The garlands of flowers around their necks began to wilt and fade. Dust blew in across the marble floors and dulled their glittering garments as they waited – all except the four gods. They stayed dry and fresh and perfect.

Damayanti raised her eyes and stared once more at the five Nalas. Four stared back at her unblinking, for gods never blink, but the fifth Nala moved his eyelids. Four had skins as dry as baked clay, but the fifth's face trickled with moisture. Across the floor, the shadows of the waiting rajahs fell in sharp, black patterns. All except for four Nalas who cast no shadows.

Damayanti's heart was filled with hope as she recognized the signs of the gods. She looked for the final proof. Slowly she lowered her eyes to their sandalled feet. Four pairs of feet floated, just a little way off the ground, but the fifth Nala stood firmly on the marble floor. With a cry of joy, Damayanti ran forward and flung her garland round his neck. "King Nala! I choose you!"

The happy couple bowed in homage before the Four Guardians of the Earth and begged for their blessings. One by one, the four gods gave their blessing and a gift.

Indra gave Nala the gift of overcoming all obstacles; Agni gave him the power over fire, and power over the three worlds, Heaven, Earth and the Underworld; Varuna gave him the power over water, and the power to have fresh garlands at any time; and Yama taught him all the secrets of preparing food, as well as strengthening his virtues.

Then began the pomp and celebrations of the wedding. Leaving Nala and Damayanti in the midst of great rejoicing, the Four Guardians of the Earth leaped once more into their chariots and flew through the air towards their dwelling place in the Himalayas.

Suddenly, just as the snow-white tips of the mountains came into view, they saw an evil apparition coming towards them, darkening the air. As it flew closer, the four gods recognized the demon, Kali. With him was his evil spirit companion, Dwapara.

Wondering what they were up to, Indra, the mighty fighter of the Drought Demons and champion dragon killer, stood up in his chariot and hailed them.

"Where are you off to, Kali, and you, Dwapara?"

Kali's evil face glinted with cunning. "We are off to Damayanti's swayamvara. I want her for my bride."

Indra and the other Guardians of the Earth roared with laughter. "You're too late, Kali! The ceremony is over – and even though she could have had the choice of one of the gods, she put her garland round the neck of a mortal – Nala! We were there – and saw it!"

Kali ground his teeth with fury. "Then is she not doomed? Has she not shown contempt for the gods, that she chose a mortal – and in your presence?"

"Don't worry, Kali," smiled the gods. "We gladly gave our consent, for Damayanti has freely chosen a mortal whom she loves and who is as worthy as one of us."

Seeing Kali's bitter anger, Indra warned him. "Stay away, Kali. Anyone who tries to curse Nala will himself be cursed and thrown into the lake of hell." Then the four gods continued on their way home.

"Huh!" roared Kali, as he watched the four chariots disappear among the mountain peaks. "They think they will have all the power! They think they can laugh. I will have my revenge. There is no mortal who is equal to any god or demon. I will find a way of entering Nala's body – and then he will be doomed." He turned his malignant face to his spirit companion. "You, Dwapara. You will help me. It is known that Nala has a passion for playing the dice. You will enter the dice – and together we will destroy him."

The evil pair then turned their chariot towards the kingdom of Nishadha to await the return home of Nala and Damayanti.

CHAPTER FOUR
Kali's Revenge

As THE GOLDEN SWAN HAD FORETOLD, Nala and Damayanti were the perfect couple. For twelve glorious years they lived in joy and happiness. They had two children, a beautiful daughter called Indrasena and a handsome boy called Indrasen. It seemed there could be no end to their good fortune.

Yet from the very beginning, disaster was only a step away. The evil Kali and his wicked companion Dwapara hovered close and invisible to the innocent king. They were in the air he breathed; the food he ate; the ground beneath his feet. They watched and waited for the one false move – the one impure act which would give Kali entry into Nala's soul.

How was it possible for Nala not to sense this terrible presence which marked every move he made? Did he never shudder as Kali leered over his shoulder? Never hesitate before stepping between the slanting shafts of sunlight which fell across the courtyard? In the darkest hour of the night, was there no warning in his dreams of the evil waiting to destroy him?

Instead, Nala seemed to thrive and grow in goodness and love. He ruled his kingdom with justice and compassion, and every day thanked the gods for his happiness. Then, the moment came that Kali had been waiting for all those twelve years – the one impure act was committed. In a hurry to go to prayers, Nala sipped water but forgot to wash his feet. Like a pebble dropping into a calm lake, shivers rippled across his body as the evil Kali triumphantly entered his soul.

Damayanti saw his eyes cloud over as if some veil had been drawn across. "My lord?" she cried, anxiously taking his arm. "You shuddered as if a fever gripped you suddenly. Is something wrong?"

Nala roughly shook off his wife's hand. "Wrong? Of course not. I only have a sudden yearning to play dice. Yes – today I'll play dice with my brother, Puskara.

I'll play him for high stakes." His eyes glinted with madness. "My brother has always been jealous of me. He would like my kingdom, my wealth, my chariots. He would like you too, Damayanti!" He turned tormented eyes on his beloved wife.

Damayanti stared in horror and disbelief at the change that had come over her husband. She ran to call his physician, certain he was ill. But it was no use. Though physicians, holy men, his counsellors of state and his best friends gathered round to help, Nala rudely dismissed them all. "Bring Puskara," he ordered. "Today I wish to play dice."

Puskara came falteringly before his brother, and the evil demon whispered in his ear. "Now's your chance, Puskara. Challenge your brother. Throw dice with the king and I will help you to win a kingdom!"

So Puskara tossed the dice onto the floor and challenged Nala. In that moment, the wicked dwarf, Dwapara, entered the dice. The two brothers began to play. They played all day and all through the night. Nala first staked his jewels, and lost them; then his golden treasures, and lost them. The game went on into the next day, and the next night, and on into the next day. Nala staked his royal garments, and his servants and slaves, and still the game went on. Rumours spread throughout the city, people gathered anxiously at the palace gates. "King Nala is ill – or mad," they whispered. But still the game went on. His counsellors shook him, and implored him to stop. Damayanti fell at his feet and begged him to consider the shame and sorrow he was bringing upon her and the children. But still the game went on. He staked his palace and hunting lodges, he staked his weapons and armies, and now he staked his beloved stables with all his magnificent horses.

Damayanti ran in despair to Nala's faithful charioteer, Varshneya. "I beg of you," she cried. "Take my children in the chariot and drive them speedily to my father's kingdom. They will be safe there from the curse that has fallen on us. Then, Varshneya," she wept, "do not return, but go wherever you wish."

Sorrowing greatly, Varshneya took the girl, Indrasena, and the boy, Indrasen, and drove them swiftly out of the city.

Now the palace was empty – everyone and everything had either fled or been gambled away.

Damayanti wandered like a lost ghost from chamber to chamber. She prayed desperately to the gods – to the Four Guardians of the Earth – but it seemed that nothing could overcome the evil of Kali.

The game went on until Nala had lost everything. Then Puskara laughed and taunted his stricken brother. "What is left to you, Nala? What else can we play for? What is your stake?"

Nala shook his head in torment.

"You have nothing," sneered Puskara, "except Damayanti. Shall we play for her?" But all the evil of Kali couldn't completely blot out the love Nala had for Damayanti. Wearily he stood up and one by one stripped the clothes from his body until he was naked. Then silently, he walked from the chamber. The game was over.

The people of Nishadha fell back in anguish as their beloved king walked through the city to the outer gates. Following closely was Damayanti. Was this really the princess with the mark of Brahma on her brow? "Oh, Mighty Creator, the Lord of all Living Things, the First Cause of Everything, how can you let your daughter be treated so?" They reached out. They would have helped, but behind them Puskara was already issuing a decree. "I am now Rajah of Nishadha!" he proclaimed. "And hear this all of you. Whoever gives food or drink to Nala shall be put to death immediately."

Horrified, Nala's sorrowing subjects watched their king and queen leave the city and wander out into the wilderness like beggars.

For three days and three nights Nala and Damayanti wandered about in desolation, drinking from streams and plucking the wild berries for food. At last they stood at a point where the path forked. One path led into the thick of the jungle, the other ran towards the south, towards the kingdom of King Bhima.

"There is nothing but shame in my company, Damayanti," said Nala with a heavy heart. "Take this path, and go home."

But Damayanti would not abandon her lord. "When misfortune and misery is greatest, is not that the very time when you most need your wife?" she argued. "I will return home to my kingdom if you will come with me. My father would welcome us both, and we could live happily there with our children."

"I can never show my face in your father's court

naked and disgraced. Oh, Damayanti! What have I done to you?"

Comforting him as best she could, Damayanti stayed at Nala's side. Together they stumbled on into the forest, until at last they fell exhausted onto the hard ground and slept.

But Kali, the evil demon, was still not satisfied with the havoc he had brought about. Seeing Damayanti's devotion to Nala was more than he could bear. His revenge would not be complete until he had wrenched them apart. He entered into Nala's dreams, brought him awake with tormented thoughts. "Leave her, leave her," whispered the wicked creature. "You will only destroy her too. Leave her."

Racked with doubt, Nala tried to resist. How could he leave his helpless wife alone in the dangerous forest?

"She will go home and be safe," urged the demon. "Leave her, leave her."

Unable to shake the evil from him, Nala rose and stared, distracted, at his innocent wife. Time and time again he left her side, only to return again. He tried to stay with her and protect her as he knew he should, but time and time again Kali lured him away. At last, Nala gave in to the demon and fled like a wild beast into the depths of the undergrowth.

A fearful silence hung over the forest. Although dawn was spreading across the sky, the birds hushed their dawn chorus, not daring to waken Damayanti. The snake slithered silently among the roots of the trees. The monkeys huddled dumbly in the branches. A watchful eagle swept a silent circle in the sky.

Suddenly, a fierce cry of sorrow stunned the forest. Damayanti had awoken. Helplessly, the forest watched her running to and fro screaming for Nala. She plunged into the long, sharp grass. The deer scattered before her. Water buffalo raised their mournful faces and watched her desperate figure as she ran blindly, calling, "Nala! Nala!"

She stood before the gleaming tiger. "Have you seen Nala?" she asked fearlessly. But the tiger just turned sadly away and padded towards the river. She ran on and on until she came to a high mountain. "Have you seen Nala?" she cried. Her voice echoed around the gulleys and ravines, but no answer came back.

All that day she ran, calling and weeping. Then as

night came, she saw the glow of fires burning through the trees. In a sacred grove, a group of hermits murmured prayers and kindled the holy flames. Damayanti stood before them wild and sorrowful. "I seek Nala," she wept.

The hermits gazed at her with calm, kind faces. "Fear not, Damayanti," they said. "You will find Nala." Then they disappeared. Her strength gone, Damayanti curled up near the glowing embers, and fell asleep at last.

In another part of the jungle, Nala staggered, demented and confused. Night fell for Nala too, and all the terrors of the forest closed in on him. He heard the howlings of jackals and the low, menacing grunts of the leopard.

Suddenly, through the dark tangle of entwined creepers and branches, he saw a great fire burning, and a voice called out, "Nala! Nala!" He plunged towards the flames. They leaped high and sharp, searing through the treetops. Again the voice called. "Nala! Nala! Save me!"

There in the very cavernous heart of the furnace, a great serpent writhed and contorted in agony, yet did not burn up.

"I am Karkotaka, King of the Serpents. I have been cursed, oh Nala, and only you can save me. Rescue me, oh mighty rajah, and I will use all my powers to help you."

Calling on Agni, the God of Fire, to protect him, Nala leaped into the flames. He coiled the writhing body round his own and brought Karkotaka out of that terrible heat and laid him on a cool, grassy bank. Behind them, the crackling fire died down, and the serpent said, "Thank you, Nala! The spell is broken. Now I will help you. Do as I say and I promise you, good fortune will come. First, walk nine steps."

Wearily, Nala walked nine steps, and stopped. Karkotaka swooped round him, and opening his fanged jaws, bit him.

With a desperate cry, Nala found himself transformed into a crooked, hunchbacked dwarf. "Is this how you repay me, oh Karkotaka?" groaned Nala despairingly.

"Don't worry," said the serpent king. "My poison will not harm you, but it will infect Kali, who dwells in you. Soon he will leave you for ever."

"In return, must I be doomed to live in this poor, crooked body?" wept Nala.

"Trust me," soothed Karkotaka. "In this guise, no one will recognize you. You can only regain Damayanti and your kingdom by playing the dice once more. You must go to the Rajah of Rituparna. There is none so skilled at dice as he. Go under the name of Vahuka, a charioteer. The rajah loves horses. He will admire your skill and want to learn from you. In exchange he will teach you the arts of playing dice. I promise you, you will regain everything you have lost."

As the poor, bent king limped away, Karkotaka called out. "Wait, Nala! I have one more gift for you." Nala turned and received a cloak from the serpent king. "When you wish to resume your true shape, wear this robe, and immediately everyone will recognize you." Then the serpent slid away into the depths of the jungle, and Nala turned his face towards the kingdom of the Rajah of Rituparna.

CHAPTER FIVE
The Homecoming

BENEATH THE ANCIENT BRANCHES of a sacred tree, King Bhima sat deep in prayer. How many prayers and tears had this old tree heard whispered among its dark leaves? How many hymns of praise and joy after a prayer was answered? Remember the day when Damayanti was born? King Bhima shuddered to his soul. Where was she, his beloved daughter? Where was Nala – that noble king so beloved of the gods? Even now, King Bhima's messengers were scouring the countryside and neighbouring kingdoms, looking for them. Surely they must be found soon? With heavy heart, the king completed his prayers and walked through the darkness towards the river. Dawn was barely a faint, thin, grey crack in the sky, yet the sound of young voices drifted towards him, and the sound of splashing water. Standing up to their waists in the holy river were two young children. As they scooped water over their naked bodies, he could hear their whispered prayers. "Oh Lord God, the Creator of all Living Things, bring back our mother and father to us." Then each child sank beneath the surface of the water, only to rise up again with uplifted arms. "Let the sins of our parents be washed away by their children. If you need a sacrifice, take us!"

Choking with tears, King Bhima watched his two grandchildren, Indrasena and Indrasen, beseeching the gods to return their parents to them. What gods could be deaf to such tender and innocent voices?

That day, an excited messenger galloped into King Bhima's palace. Exhausted and covered with dust, he fell from his horse and cried, "I have found Damayanti!" King Bhima quietly led the messenger to his inner chamber, and listened to the news which was brought to him.

"In my searching," said the messenger, "I came to the kingdom of Chedi. I had heard tales of a mysterious woman who the queen mother had pitied. She had brought her into the palace to be handmaiden to her own daughter, Princess Sunanda. Some said she was mad, for her skin was always stained dark, and her hair hung long and wild; and yet, my lord, if you looked full into her face, was there ever such true beauty. Though ravaged with sorrow and untold pain, such goodness and truth gleamed in her dark eyes, like a moon hiding behind the storm clouds. I tried to find out more about her, but no one knew who she was or where she came from. Only that she had followed a caravan train out of the jungle, and that she must be high-born as she would only eat food prepared by Brahmans. I told them about Damayanti, and said there was one sure proof that would identify her, the mark of Brahma above her left eyebrow. But who could tell with her face so stained, and masked under her long hair?

"The queen mother went to the woman and said, 'If you are Damayanti, then you are my own sister's daughter. I saw you once as a young child. Wipe away the stains so that we may behold the mark of Brahma on your brow, and know that it is truly you.'"

"I myself wiped away the stain," whispered the messenger.

King Bhima, who all this time had been listening with half-closed eyes, slowly opened them and fixed them on the messenger.

"And…" he whispered. "Did you see it?"

"Yes, my lord, I saw it. It is she. I have found Damayanti."

Damayanti is found! Once more her name sped round the palace and into the towns and villages. It was as though she had been born again. Damayanti has been found, and she is coming home.

It was a joyous homecoming. Flags and garlands festooned the houses and streets; elephants, camels, horses and bullocks were painted and decorated for the occasion. Musicians and dancers whirled and twirled as Damayanti was brought home in her father's chariot. How she was embraced and wept over by her father and mother – and how she hugged and kissed her son and daughter, Indrasen and Indrasena. But everyone knew that nothing could wipe away the sorrow imprinted on her face until Nala too was found and they were both restored to each other.

Although King Bhima's messengers were still searching for Nala, Damayanti decided to send out her own messengers. They were to proclaim these words: "Where is the gambler who abandoned his wife in the forest alone and unprotected? Who stole her clothes, as she lay sleeping, to cover his own nakedness? She is home now, weeping and waiting for him to return. Have pity, noble hero, and come back."

Day after day, Damayanti's lonely figure stood on her balcony, from where she could see the road into the city. As each weary messenger returned, how eagerly she ran to greet them, and how they loathed to shake their heads and see the hope fade from her eyes. Then one day, the Brahman, Parnada, one of the king's most devoted messengers, came riding in. He had ridden day and night, and so it was dawn when he galloped into the palace courtyard. Damayanti was at prayer, but when she had finished and got up to go once more onto the balcony, she saw Parnada waiting patiently between the pillars. Her heart leaped. "Have you news?" she asked faintly.

"I had a strange encounter in the city of Ayodhya," said the Brahman carefully. "After I had proclaimed your message an ugly, crooked man came before me. He was the royal charioteer in the service of the Rajah of

Rituparna. His name, he said, was Vahuka – and indeed his amazing skill with horses was spoken of throughout the land. He was also famous for preparing food; King Rituparna will eat no one else's."

"Nala was famous for these skills too," thought Damayanti feverishly. "Tell me more," she begged. "What had he to say to you?"

He spoke these words sorrowing greatly. "If a wife is faithful, even though she has been deserted and left naked by her husband, she will not give in to anger or revenge, but will remain true to her lord who has been robbed of his kingdom and his happiness."

When Damayanti heard these words, she wept. She was certain that somehow this hunchbacked charioteer known as Vahuka was her own dear lord, Nala. "I must find a way to make him come home," she cried. "I have a plan, Parnada. Go back to Ayodhya and tell the Rajah of Rituparna that Bhima's daughter will once more hold a swayamvara. Tomorrow at dawn she will choose her new husband, for no one knows if Nala is alive or dead. Go now!"

News of Damayanti's second swayamvara filled the Rajah of Rituparna with excitement. He was resolved to go. "Hurry, Vahuka!" he shouted. "We have but one single day to get to King Bhima's kingdom for Damayanti's swayamvara! Only you are skilled enough to get me there on time."

Bursting with doubt and grief, Nala yoked together four of the finest, swiftest steeds and made ready the chariot. Then with a flick of the reins he and the rajah set off at a gallop. At first the horses' hooves hammered down the road, pounding like wedding drums. The chariot flew along faster and faster, so swift and smooth that it seemed the horses' hooves could no longer be on the ground. The rajah gazed in amazement and admiration at the hunchbacked charioteer. The way he stood holding the reins, he seemed almost godlike.

The chariot flew on, as smooth as a swan, over rocky hills, through dense forest, across surging rivers and jungle swamps. Yet it was as if the chariot had wings, for the rajah felt no bump or sway, but only the wind whistling through his hair. How he longed to learn Vahuka's skills.

Suddenly there loomed up before them a great tree whose branches overhung their path. "Vahuka!" shouted the rajah. "You are a matchless charioteer, no one save the gods has your skill with horses. But I have a skill too which is unmatched on this earth. There is no one who knows the art of numbers better than I. See that tree? I'm willing to wager that on those two branches overhanging the road there are fifty million leaves, and two thousand and ninety-five berries."

The old gambling instinct gripped Nala's soul. He pulled up the horses in a cloud of dust.

"Count the berries!" urged the rajah. "If I am right, teach me your power over the horses, and in return I'll tell you all my secrets with numbers and dice. Believe me, you will never lose another game of dice!"

The hot afternoon seemed frozen in time as Nala counted the leaves and berries, and saw that the rajah was right. Did the gods halt the spinning of the globe while the Rajah of Rituparna taught Nala everything he knew about numbers, and the secret arts of throwing the dice? As Nala grew to understand, and the secret knowledge entered his soul, he began to shudder. His stomach heaved as he stumbled about, his body racked with convulsions. Then as he opened his mouth in a terrible cry of agony, the evil Kali and the serpent's venom passed out of his body. At last Nala was free!

He gave a shout of joy. "Come, my lord! Let us continue speedily, and on the way I will teach you all there is to know about horses! We mustn't be late for the swayamvara of the peerless Damayanti!"

All through the night they galloped, and all through the night the rajah learned the skills of his charioteer, Vahuka. It was not yet dawn when the sounds of Nala's thundering chariot reached the city of King Bhima. A tremor ran through the palace. The elephants raised their trunks and trumpeted, the horses stamped and neighed in their stables, and the peacocks on the palace walls fanned out their tails and danced, as though Indra had come with the rains.

There was a flurry of activity in the courtyard: servants carrying oil lamps came running to help their visitors. Grooms led away the panting horses and King Bhima came hurrying to welcome the Rajah of Rituparna.

But Damayanti had eyes only for the strange hunchbacked charioteer. She sent her handmaiden to watch him. "Tell me everything you see," she ordered.

Although King Bhima offered his guest a meal, the Rajah of Rituparna asked that Vahuka, his own charioteer, should be taken to the kitchens, where he would prepare food. The handmaiden watched closely as Vahuka went to the low dwellings. How could a charioteer prepare a meal for his master? In the middle of the night the cooks lay sleeping, the water pitchers were empty and the fires out.

Vahuka approached the low doorway to the kitchen. To the handmaiden's amazement, instead of stooping low to enter as everyone did, the doorway grew and grew until he could walk through upright like a warrior. Creeping up to the doorway to peer inside, the handmaiden saw Vahuka raise an empty pitcher, and lo – it was brimming with water. Then the hunchback knelt before the cold, dead grate and held out some withered grass. There was a crackle and a flash, and a fire sprang up with darting flames. Then Vahuka went humbly to the little shrine to give thanks to the gods. Yesterday's offerings of flowers had dried and faded, but when the hunchback lightly touched them, they bloomed once more, fresh and colourful, and their scent filled the air.

Damayanti's handmaiden didn't stop to see any more. Gasping with excitement, she rushed back to the princess to tell her all that she had seen.

Damayanti knelt in thankfulness. Nala was here, using the gifts which the Four Guardians of the Earth had given him on his wedding day. Then she asked her father, King Bhima, to have Vahuka brought before her.

The Rajah of Rituparna was puzzled. What kind of swayamvara was this that his charioteer should be summoned before Damayanti? And where were all the other suitors?

The crooked hunchback stood with bowed head before Damayanti. As a rosy dawn flooded across the grey sky, Damayanti picked up her freshly strung garland and, brimming with tears, walked steadily up to Vahuka and placed it round his neck. "Take once more the daughter of King Bhima to be your wife," she murmured.

A soft wind rustled through the palace chambers, and it seemed as though the air was filled with the sound of singing voices and the scent of flowers. Vahuka then took the robe which the serpent king, Karkotaka, had given him. He put it round his shoulders, and immediately, the hunchbacked charioteer disappeared, and there in his place stood King Nala.

They embraced, and such rejoicing echoed through

the land. Banners and garlands were hung from street to street and door to door. Now there was just one task more to be completed. With Damayanti at his side, King Nala rode back to his kingdom. He had one final game to play, but this time he carried with him the secret powers of the dice.

News travelled ahead of them. As Nala and Damayanti entered their own kingdom, silent, fearful crowds lined the streets. How they longed to welcome back their beloved king and queen, but how they feared Nala's brother, Puskara.

Nala rode boldly into the palace courtyard. He stood up in the chariot and shouted loudly for his brother to come out. "Puskara! I have come to challenge you. This time the stake is Damayanti herself. Come, brother! Come and throw the dice with me, and let the winner take all!"

Puskara appeared. Haughty and overconfident with power, he was greedy for Damayanti. So sure of himself was he, as he rubbed the dice gleefully in his hands and arrogantly tossed it into the ring. Then Nala tossed the dice – and with one throw, he won back all that he had lost.

The kingdom exploded with rejoicing and happiness as Nala and Damayanti were restored to their people. "We were all in the grip of the evil demon, Kali," cried Nala. "Let us put the past behind us and forgive each other." Then he embraced his own brother and gave him a kingdom of his own to rule.

So once more peace and prosperous happiness returned to the land, and Nala and Damayanti ruled for many long years with goodness and justice.

Up in their heavens, the gods looked down and smiled with contentment and showered the world with petals and raindrops.

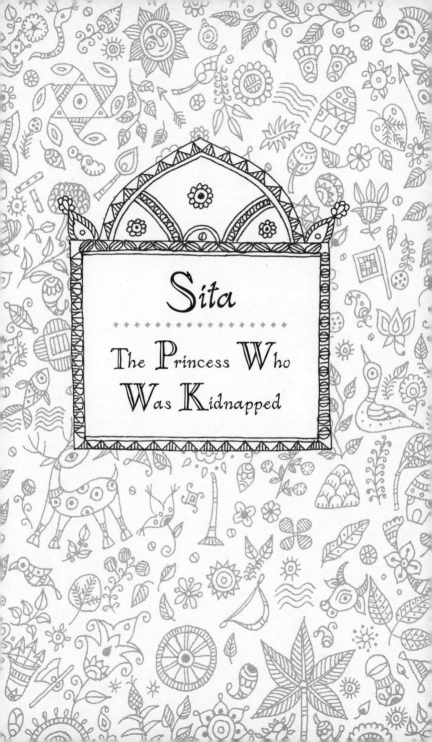

Sita

◆◆◆◆◆◆◆

The Princess Who Was Kidnapped

CHAPTER ONE
The Bow of Shiva

KING JANAKA, the rich and powerful ruler of Mithila, rode out of his city one morning just before dawn. He rode alone and no one dared to ask him where he was going. The guards at the city gate watched discreetly as the unarmed, unprotected king cantered down the grey road into the countryside.

He was soon out of sight as the road burrowed between deep fields of mustard and of green, sprouting wheat. He zigzagged through clumps of mango and guava groves, and wound his way in and out of banana plantations and citrus trees.

At last, as the red sun rose over the horizon, he reached a field in which nothing grew. It was rough and barren and full of stones. Nearby, there lay a disused plough. The king dismounted here, and tethered his horse beneath a tree. He walked over to the plough. It was old and rough and heavy, but the king bent down and heaved it into position. He dragged the plough all the way down the field. When he looked back, gasping, and panting with exhaustion, he saw that he had made one deep, straight furrow. He gave a small smile of pride and dragged the plough back up the field. Up and down he went all day, singing hymns of praise to the gods to give him strength and courage.

The sun arched upwards through the sky and reached its burning zenith, but still the king didn't stop. Up and down he went, dragging the plough, until at last, as the sun was dipping below the trees, the whole field was divided up into neat, straight furrows, ready for planting. The king threw aside the plough and spat on his blistered hands. A flock of egrets rose white and long-legged into the pink sky. As they circled and flew away, the king looked around him uncertainly. He had obeyed the gods and ploughed a field with his own bare hands. Would he now get the reward he had been praying for all these years? Suddenly, he heard a faint cry. At first he could see nothing except the newly ploughed field and his horse munching on the long grass. He heard another cry. The king ran down between the furrows looking this way and that. Suddenly – there it was. Lying in the depth of a furrow, as though the plough had just turned it up, was a tiny, naked, brown baby girl. The king fell on his knees with joy beside this earthy cradle. The gods had granted his wish and given him a child. Gently, he gathered her up into his cloak and galloped back to the palace. He handed the small, dusty bundle to his queen and cried, "I begged the gods for a child. I performed every penance, made every pilgrimage. Then they told me, if I ploughed a field with my own hands, I would be rewarded. Today I ploughed that field – and look!"

Trembling with amazement, the queen unwrapped the cloak. "It's as though she was born out of the earth itself!" she murmured. "Let us call her 'Sita' which means 'child of Mother Earth'."

The king and queen were overjoyed with their daughter, Sita. They loved her with all their hearts, and Sita grew up with all the beauty, grace and goodness of a goddess. Indeed, Sita was so special that King Janaka knew that she, a gift of the gods, could not marry any ordinary mortal. Somewhere there must be a man who was of equal nobility and goodness as she. But the question was – who? And how could he be recognized?

Then King Janaka remembered the bow of Shiva. This bow had been handed down in his family from generation to generation. The bow of this mighty god was so massive that it took a team of men to move it. King Janaka proclaimed that the man who could lift Shiva's bow single-handed and string it would be the man who won his daughter, Sita, for his wife.

The mightiest of kings, princes and warriors came from all over the land to try and lift the bow. How they heaved and sweated, but to no avail. Shiva's bow was as immovable and solid as a rock, and the strongest of men departed exhausted with the effort, and weeping with frustration.

One day, as Sita was wandering in her garden, she heard a buzz of excited voices in the courtyard of the palace. Full of curiosity, she ran up the steps to her balcony and gazed down, unseen through the fine, marble tracery. A holy man in saffron robes, with long, white matted hair and beard, waited at the entrance.

Although he was old, he stood upright and powerful, and his face was lined with wisdom and experience. She heard his name murmured: "Vishwamitra!" Was this really the great sage, Vishwamitra? He was supposed to be the wisest man in the land, a counsellor of kings and a teacher of princes. On either side of him stood two tall, slender young men. They both carried bows slung across their shoulders and a sheath of arrows hung down their backs. Sita gazed at them and felt strangely disturbed. Though they were young, they had a look about them that was as courageous and fearless as tigers. The older one, especially, had such proud bearing and handsome nobility that Sita's heart was moved.

Vishwamitra was welcomed by King Janaka with warmth and humility, and then asked, "Who are these young men who accompany you?"

"These young men," answered the holy man with pride, "are the sons of King Dasratha of Ayodhya. Prince Rama and his younger brother, Prince Lakshmana. They are my pupils. I have taught them all I know – and though still young, they are learned in all the vedas and holy incantations; they have mastered the warrior's skills of archery, horse-riding and warfare; they have killed many demons and are blessed by the gods. Now, if it may please you, Your Majesty, Prince Rama and Prince Lakshmana would like to see the great bow of Shiva."

When it was known that these were the sons of King Dasratha, the whole city turned out to try and catch a glimpse of the two young princes. Their fame had travelled throughout the land and many thought that Rama was more like a god than a man. It was whispered that he was an incarnation of Vishnu himself.

Sita, gazing down secretly on the scene, felt a rush of tears. Would Prince Rama try to lift the bow? She had seen many stronger men try, indeed gods and giants had come before the great bow, but none had managed to lift even one end. Sadly she watched her father lead Vishwamitra and the two princes towards the great hall. Just before the holy man passed between the golden pillars, he suddenly lifted his head. He seemed to look straight at her, although Sita knew that she was completely hidden. Then he turned and was out of sight.

A quiver of excitement ran through the great hall. Everyone was jostling and straining to see the two princes – the sons of King Dasratha. King Janaka sent for the great bow, though it was only to please Vishwamitra. He didn't believe the two princes could do any more than look at the famous bow.

Soon a rumbling and clattering was heard. The doors were flung open, and everyone fell back as an immense, iron, eight-wheeled chariot was hauled in by a team of the strongest warriors. Across the chariot lay Shiva's bow. There was an awed hush as they stood before the celestial weapon. King Janaka touched it reverently. "Come! Look! This mighty bow has been guarded by my family for generations. Whoever lifts it and bends the bow can have my daughter, Sita, for a wife – but many fine warriors have tried and failed, and even the gods are in awe of it."

Prince Rama and Prince Lakshmana gazed at the bow for a long time, then just as the king was about to wave it away, Prince Rama said very quietly and politely, "Would Your Majesty permit me to lift the bow and string it?"

There was a gasp of amazement from the watching crowd. King Janaka opened his mouth to protest, but caught Vishwamitra's eye, and gulped instead. "Er ... of course, you may ... try ... but..."

With a quiet smile, Prince Rama stepped forward and lifted the bow with his left hand. Then with his right hand, he bent the bow and strung it as easily as if it were a musical instrument. But he didn't stop there. He went on bending and bending the bow, until like a thunder clap, it snapped in two. The sound shook the earth, and everyone fell terror-stricken to the ground.

King Janaka bowed low before Rama. "Whoever you are, be you man or a god in disguise, I willingly give you Sita. Your names shall be linked for ever; they shall be murmured in prayer and sung about in hymns. Rama, Sita, Sita, Rama – all fathers will wish for sons like Rama, and all mothers for daughters like Sita. Let the wedding celebrations begin immediately!"

So Rama received Sita as his wife as joyfully as the great god Vishnu received his queen Lakshmi, and there was rejoicing throughout the land.

CHAPTER TWO
Exile

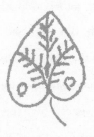

THE CITY OF AYODHYA was humming with excitement as they waited for Prince Rama to come home with his beautiful new wife. As the couple rode into the city they were surrounded by cheering crowds. Garlands were tossed before them, and flowers rained down on them from the rooftops and balconies.

Waiting at the palace was the royal household and King Dasratha's three queens and their sons: Queen Kausalaya, the chief queen and Rama's mother; Queen Sumitra, mother of Lakshmana and Satrughna; and Queen Kaikeyi, mother of Bharata. Fondly, they embraced Rama and Sita with such love and warmth, festooning them with scented garlands and sprinkling rose water at their feet. Then the three queens led Sita away to be bathed and rested, and from the very beginning they loved her, and drew her into the family.

But there was one evil heart who felt no love. A wizened, old nurse called Manthara had cared for Queen Kaikeyi's son, Bharata. She loved Bharata with a passion, but it was equalled with a passionate hatred and jealousy of Rama. She loathed to see his popularity and his happiness. For years now, she had been watching and waiting for a way to harm him. Now that Rama was home and with such a fine wife as Sita, old King Dasratha began to think about giving up his kingly duties. He wanted to retire to a monastery and spend the rest of his days in prayer and meditation. "Let my eldest son, Rama, take my place as king," he told his counsellors. "Rama is young and strong, and has all the wisdom and strength to be a fine leader." The counsellors were very enthusiastic, and when the people of the city heard the news, they went wild with delight. All the queens and Rama's brothers were glad to see the burdens of state lifted from their beloved old king and placed in such good hands. But the evil nurse, Manthara, ground her teeth with fury. "Rama must not be king," she hissed.

Preparations for the handing-over ceremony began immediately. Now that the decision was made, the old king wanted Rama to be king the very next day. People rushed into the streets with flags and banners, decorating all the walls and balconies. Queen Kaikeyi had wandered up on to the roof to get a view of the festivities below. She laughed and sang, as bands of musicians jigged through the streets with thunderous drumming and wild wind instruments piercing the air. The evil Manthara sidled up to her, and spoke in snake-like tones. "I don't know what you're so pleased about. How can you bear to be under Rama's command? And what about Queen Kausalaya, and that slip of a girl, Sita? Are you to be at their beck and call too?"

Queen Kaikeyi shook her head sadly. "Why do you hate Rama so much?" she cried. "After all, he is the eldest son, and he has always shown me the same love and respect that he shows his own mother. He knows that I am King Dasratha's favourite wife. He would never harm me."

"You fool!" sneered the wicked nurse. "That's exactly why he hates you. As soon as he's king – you see – everything will change. He'll send your son, Bharata, into exile – or even have him killed. Are you so blind that you can't see that? Only you can save him."

Queen Kaikeyi clasped her head in anguish. Could this be true? She wanted to block her ears and not listen to the poison pouring from the old nurse's mouth, but it was too late. The seeds of hatred and doubt were sown, and sank deep into her heart. The old nurse went on whispering. "Go on, save him! You can do it. The old king is besotted with you. He never has been able to resist your beauty. Remember, he owes you a favour. Now's the time to claim it. You saved his life after a battle, and he promised you two boons, did he not? He cannot refuse you."

"What shall I ask him?" stammered the queen.

"Why, tell him to make your son, Bharata, king instead of Rama. Rama must be exiled for a long time. Go now, before it's too late." The evil woman pushed the hesitant queen towards the steps down into the royal chamber.

The hatred and jealousy which the old nurse had breathed into Queen Kaikeyi was now mixed with a burning ambition. Yes, why not? Why shouldn't her son, Bharata, be king? Wasn't he as good and noble as

Rama? She hurried down towards King Dasratha's chamber, leaving the sounds of rejoicing scattering up into the night air.

King Dasratha was at prayer when Queen Kaikeyi entered his chamber. But he didn't mind being disturbed. He turned to embrace his favourite wife, his beautiful wife whom he adored, but was shocked to see her looking so tormented.

"What is it?" he asked anxiously. "Is something wrong? Tell me immediately. There is nothing on this earth that I wouldn't do to make you happy."

"There are two things you can do," cried Kaikeyi, "and indeed if you do not do them I shall surely die."

"Tell me what it is, and it shall be done," promised the king.

"It is my wish that you install Bharata as king at the ceremony tomorrow, and it is my second wish that you exile Rama into the forest. He should be stripped of all his worldly goods and live as a poor hermit for fourteen years."

"Are you mad?" King Dasratha stared in disbelief, the blood draining from his face.

"I am not mad. You owe me these boons. Remember

your promise when I saved your life?" retorted Kaikeyi.

"I remember," whispered Dasratha hoarsely. "But you can't mean it."

"I mean it – or else I die," replied the queen.

King Dasratha fell shuddering to the floor and clasped her feet. All night long he wept and pleaded, but Kaikeyi remained icy and hard, and nothing would move her.

"Oh, let the dawn never come and reveal your wickedness," cried the king brokenly.

But the dawn did come. The preparations for the ceremony were ready. His chief counsellor came knocking at the chamber to fetch the king. He was startled to be met at the door by Queen Kaikeyi. "King Dasratha wishes to see Prince Rama here immediately," she informed him with an imperious voice. "Bring him here at once."

Alarmed by the message, Prince Rama galloped through the city from the Vishnu temple where he had spent the night in prayer. He galloped right through the courtyard and along the palace walks which led to his father's chamber. Leaping from his horse he rushed inside to find his father.

Meanwhile, in her chamber, Sita was being dressed for the ceremony which would make her queen. Her long black hair was threaded with pearls and knotted with freshly plucked flowers; a gold chain parted her hair down the middle and linked up on either side with the droplets of pearls and emeralds which hung from her ears; another loop of gold chain linked up to a diamond stud glittering in her nose. More jewels and golden chains criss-crossed her silken bodice and hung over her hips. A gold and silver threaded silk saree was gathered round her waist as a shimmering skirt. Then her feet and hands were intricately decorated with fine red patterns; rings were slipped on to her fingers and toes, and golden anklets at her feet; and they slid bangles of gold up her wrists and arms – so that there was hardly any part of her body which wasn't richly adorned. As she stood there, glowing in all her finery, even her handmaidens fell back in awe, for she looked more like a goddess than a queen.

Outside, the clamour of excitement rose. Now crowds were surging round the palace. They climbed onto walls and up trees; they leaned over balconies and terraces and clustered on roofs. Expectation sizzled in the air as they waited for the procession to begin.

Suddenly the door was flung open, and there was Rama. Sita turned, full of smiles – then froze. Rama stood like a statue, his face hard and expressionless. Behind him, a group of counsellors whispered in agitation, and there was a sound of weeping. Rama came forward. As his eyes took her into his gaze, they softened with love and anguish.

"Dearest Sita, I have come to say farewell."

Sita controlled the panic that swelled up inside her. She clenched her fists to stop the trembling that swept over her. "Where must you go, my lord?" she asked calmly.

"It is my father's wish that my brother Bharata be made king instead of me. It is also his wish that I go into exile in the forest and live as a simple hermit for fourteen years. These two boons he has granted Queen Kaikeyi in return for her having saved his life."

Sorrow and lamentation filled the palace. It overflowed into the streets and swept like a flood all through the city. Suddenly, celebration turned to confusion and anger. There were shouts of, "Kill Queen Kaikeyi! Kill Bharata! Rama is our king! Long live

Rama!" Mobs began roaming the streets, and it seemed as if violence must tear the city apart.

The palace counsellors begged Rama not to go. "Everyone is on your side. They will say the king is too old to know what he is doing."

But Rama said, "A promise is a promise and cannot be broken. Now you must promise me…" Rama gathered his counsellors round him, and his mother, Queen Kausalaya, and Queen Sumitra and her sons, Lakshmana and Satrughna. "You must all promise me to uphold the law. You must honour and obey King Bharata. He is my beloved brother, and I know will lead you well. You must respect and obey Queen Kaikeyi." Then Rama took Sita's hand in his and looked at the gathering. "And above all, I beg of you to take care of my beloved wife."

But Sita said quietly, "I am your wife, and I promised that I would never leave your side. Your exile is my exile. I am coming with you into the forest."

Lakshmana, his brother, also stepped forward and said, "I too am going with you into exile. Alone, you will surely die, but together we can overcome the dangers."

Rama pleaded with them to change their minds, but

it was no use, so at last Rama, Sita and Lakshmana said their farewells.

Rama and Lakshmana took off their fine robes and put on the rough garments made from bark which all hermits wear. They persuaded Sita that she need not do the same. So Sita kept on her silken saree, but took off all her jewels except for her bracelets and anklets. Then the three of them went out of the palace and took the road towards the forest, leaving behind King Dasratha dying of a broken heart, and a city hushed in mourning.

CHAPTER THREE
Kidnapped

KING JATAYUS, Rajah of the Vultures, soared high and cool in the blazing, blue sky. Below him the jungle crawled vast and green like a huge monster devouring the land. It climbed up steep precipices and plunged into valleys; it clawed across the flat lands, breaking out into long, yellow tiger grass, giving way to black, muddy pools, where storks stood like statues and the hog deer tiptoed shyly down the bank to drink.

For years now King Jatayus had watched the three royal humans as they struggled to survive in the forest. He felt he was their guardian and always wanted to be ready if his help was needed. He especially watched Sita, marvelling how this delicate princess had chosen to share bitter exile with Rama.

But Jatayus was not the only one who watched Rama, Sita and Lakshmana. They had slowly travelled south, and finally stopped to build themselves a quiet forest home. Here they wished to live out the rest of their long exile – but it was here that a demon princess called Surpa-nakha discovered them.

Surpa-nakha was the sister of Ravana, the Demon King of Lanka. One day, as she swirled and crackled through the jungle – an ugly, deformed, fearsome creature – she suddenly saw Rama, and her evil heart was astounded. He was so beautiful – like a lotus, so pale and slender, and yet like a warrior or a god, with his bow slung across his back, and his proud and noble bearing. She fell in love with him. Her love transformed her, and made her grow beautiful. Then she stepped before him and said, "I am the sister of Ravana, King of the Demons. I have come before you because I love you, and I choose you for my husband. Come with me, and together we can roam the jungle and scale the mountain peaks."

Rama was startled by this lovely woman, but nothing could shake his love for Sita. In a gentle voice he told Surpa-nakha that he would never leave his beloved wife. Surpa-nakha was filled with anguished rage. She would have drunk Sita's blood if she could.

"Why not see if Lakshmana will have you," suggested Rama. "He is a noble prince."

But Lakshmana rejected her light-heartedly and wounded her pride. When Sita appeared to see what was going on, Surpa-nakha leaped at her like a blazing leopard ready to devour her. Like a flash of lightning, Lakshmana drew his sword and struck off her nose. Surpa-nakha fled, demented, like a shrieking wind, her dreadful cries echoing through the rocky jungle.

Now the sky darkened as red as blood; jackals howled and crows screamed like witches. The demons gathered for revenge.

Hastily, Rama hid Sita and Lakshmana in a cave. "Stay here," he ordered. "This is my battle and I'll fight it alone." Then he put on glowing armour, and took up his sacred bow. The arrows were already beginning to smoke as he went out to meet the demon army. He stood waiting, with godliness shining from him as the demons hurtled towards him and flaming arrows showered all around. Then Rama lifted his celestial bow and fired. The demons scattered, screaming with terror. Fitting one flaming arrow, he fired and struck dead the leader.

The battle was over. Surpa-nakha went furiously to her brother, Ravana. He swore revenge. "But revenge need not be through battle," he mused. "It will be through stealing that which is most dear to Rama!"

The forest calmed down; the red sky lightened and cleared; the silenced monkeys began chattering softly, and the birds fluttered and sang once more. The battle was won for the moment, but Rama knew this was not the last of the demons. They would surely return for revenge.

The days went by. Rama, Sita and Lakshmana continued their gentle routine of gathering wood for fuel and hunting for food. Sita spent long hours wandering nearby in the forest, collecting herbs and spices, and fresh flowers for her hair. She tried not to forget the dangers – to remember the snake lurking among the roots, or the prowling tiger lying in wait in the long grass, but there was so much beauty too. When she marvelled at the burning red flowers hanging from the creepers, or the sight of the wild peacock displaying his brilliant feathers, she could almost forget that she had once lived a life of luxury in a king's palace.

One calm day, a golden deer grazed innocently among the trees. King Jatayus saw it, as he wheeled a watchful arc overhead. As the animal moved delicately through the grass, the silver spots on its body shone like little moons, and the sapphire tips of its horns sparkled in the sunlight.

A little way off, Sita was picking flowers and singing softly to herself. She could see Rama and Lakshmana sitting outside their forest home, whittling arrows, and laughing among themselves. Suddenly, she heard a faint rustle, and found herself gazing into the blue, lotus eyes of the golden deer. It stared at her, but instead of fleeing, it just lowered its head and went on nibbling, as if there was no reason for two such beautiful creatures as themselves to be afraid of each other.

Sita ran silently back to tell Rama and Lakshmana. "Come quickly and see this amazing deer. It has the most beautiful coat I have ever seen!" cried Sita.

Rama leaped to his feet, but Lakshmana cried, "Wait, Rama! Don't go! This might be a trick. I have often heard that demons disguise themselves as fawns."

But Rama picked up his bow and said, "Don't worry, Lakshmana. I must go and see this deer. Perhaps its skin would make a worthy cloak for Sita! You both stay here, and Lakshmana, whatever you do, don't leave Sita alone." Then he was off, running low and fitting an arrow to his bowstring as he went.

Lakshmana remained, fearful and uneasy. He paced up and down inside their hut, stopping in the doorway every now and then to see if Rama was returning.

Suddenly there came a cry from the trees. "Lakshmana! Help! Come quickly!" Lakshmana froze. His first instinct was to run and help. His second instinct was to stay.

"Lakshmana! What are you waiting for?" cried Sita in a puzzled voice. "That was Rama calling you. Go, Lakshmana, go!"

"I can't leave you alone," protested Lakshmana. "Rama ordered me to stay with you."

Again Rama's voice called desperately. "Lakshmana! Lakshmana! I need your help! Oh, come quickly!"

Still Lakshmana faltered in an agony of hesitation. Sita grasped his arm, panic-stricken. "In the name of heaven, go! He must be in danger! You're his brother! Don't you care?" She dragged him to the door.

Lakshmana groaned helplessly. At last he took a

stick and drew a circle round the entrance to the hut. "I'll go and find Rama," he said. "But stay here in the hut," he pleaded. "Whatever you do, don't cross this circle. It has special powers to protect you." Then taking up his bow, and slinging his arrows across his back, Lakshmana raced towards the trees.

Sita waited, terrified and alone. As she waited, she was being watched – secretly. It was Ravana himself, the Lankan King of the Demons. This terrible, ten-headed monster watched the beautiful princess and wanted her for himself. Ten evil smiles played round his lips when he saw his plan to lure Rama and Lakshmana away had worked. It was he who had sent a demon disguised as a deer – so magical that no one who saw it could resist it. Now Sita was alone. All he had to do was persuade her to cross the magic circle.

Ravana changed himself into an old holy man, and came hobbling towards the hut with a begging bowl outstretched in his hand. He stood before the entrance, just outside the circle, and pleaded for some food.

Oh, why did Sita not look up into the sky for a single moment? She would have seen the King of the Vultures, Jatayus, plunging desperately this way and that in an effort to warn her. From his height he had seen first Rama and then Lakshmana rushing blindly through the thicket in pursuit of the golden deer. He too had heard Rama's voice calling for help, but he saw that the voice came not from Rama's throat, but from the deer. Jatayus dived down into the trees, trying to warn the brothers, then rose upwards again, streaking towards Sita to try and make her see the danger. But it was no use. Sita was already wavering before the kind-faced old holy man.

"Here, take this fruit," said Sita, holding out an offering, but staying well within the circle.

"Alas!" The holy man shook his head. "It is forbidden to receive gifts from inside a home. You must come over here and offer them to me."

Sita hesitated. She felt so lonely, so in need of comfort. Surely this kind old man would not harm her? She persuaded herself that she had nothing to fear, and smiling, crossed the circle.

With a roar of joy, Ravana sprang upon her like a tiger on its prey. His holy disguise fell away, and Sita found herself staring into twenty dreadful, blazing eyes.

Sita screamed and struggled as Ravana dragged her into his monstrous chariot, drawn by braying asses with demonic heads. But it was no use. The chariot rose into the air and Sita's screams were lost in the wind. Only Jatayus saw what happened. With a fearful shriek, this noble King of the Vultures hurled himself at the fleeing chariot in an attempt to stop it. It was a brave but futile act. As he pecked frantically at the sides of the chariot and beat his wings trying to drag it downwards, his beak was smashed and his body torn and broken. With an anguished howl, the bird plummeted down to earth and crashed into the trees.

CHAPTER FOUR
The Rescue

THE DEMONIC ASSES GALLOPED through the darkening sky pulling King Ravana's chariot. Lying, half fainting, in the back, Sita desperately pulled off her bangles and tossed them over the side. Perhaps someone would discover them and know that Sita had passed this way.

The bangles sparkled and flashed like falling stars, down, down until they were swallowed up in the dark, dense jungle below.

Now the speeding chariot flew on southwards, over the shores of the mainland. The ocean heaved, and there, far below among its billowing waves, gleaming like a fabulous jewel, lay the island of Lanka. The lights of King Ravana's palace blazed with torches, and the demons rushed to prepare a welcome for their returning king.

Exhausted with grief, Sita was asleep when the chariot landed. Demon handmaidens lifted the sleeping princess and carried her to a royal bedchamber where they laid her among silken sheets in a soft rose-scented bed.

King Ravana came and stood nearby, gazing at her full of longing. He would have bent to kiss her with his twenty lips. As if knowing his thoughts, Sita shuddered in her sleep. But Ravana knew she was the daughter of a god and protected by Brahma's curse which said, if Ravana attempted to touch any woman without her willingness, he would have all his ten heads struck off. So, planning ways of making her love him, Ravana crept from the bedchamber.

It was barely dawn next morning when Sita awoke. She lay with her eyes still closed, listening. Remembering. Was it all a terrible nightmare? Had she been kidnapped by a fearful, ten-headed demon? Or, when she had opened her eyes, would she find she was lying on a simple matting of leaves on the ground, with her beloved Rama at her side? Then she felt the soft bed beneath her body and the feel of silken sheets.

She smelt the perfumes wafting round her head and heard the low gruntings of the demons. She sat up in terror. "Rama! Rama!"

"It's no good calling for Rama, my lady," croaked a demon voice. An ugly head bent over her, half animal, half human. "Rama is far away. He'll never find you. You might as well forget him, for you'll never see him again."

Sita sprang from her bed and ran from the chamber. She could hear peals of laughter, snufflings and cacklings. She ran across crystal floors, and found herself standing at the top of a gold and silver staircase, encrusted with jewels. Down she ran, two at a time, calling, "Rama! Rama!" She fled into the courtyard, seeking escape, but the demon warriors raised their weapons, and snarled.

Suddenly a choir of voices, it seemed, spoke in one rich harmony. "Sita, oh sweet, sweet lady!" There stood King Ravana, huge and monstrous. His ten heads resplendent with ten crowns loomed over her, and from his ten mouths spoke ten voices. "Oh, golden one," they murmured, soft as bees. "Oh, beautiful maiden of coral lips, and teeth like jasmin. You are as ravishing as a solitary moon at midnight, as perfect as a goddess. You have captured my heart. Be my chief queen, dear Sita, and my empire shall be yours. Forget Rama. His worldly powers are nothing compared to mine."

Sita's eyes blazed with scorn. "You speak too surely. You do not know Rama – this godlike hero, unbeaten in battle. Beware! You do not realize how rash you've been. And what makes you think you can win me? Could you pluck the tongue of a cobra? Could you seize the sun from its heaven? Oh, foolish king! I would rather die than have you lay one finger on me."

Then Ravana heaved with rage when he saw that his honeyed words were received so scornfully. "Then you shall leave the comforts of the palace," he roared. "If you will not be my queen, be my hostage, and be guarded by my most bestial demons. One day, Rama will come looking for you, and I will take my revenge on you both!"

Ever since Sita had been kidnapped, the forest rang with Rama's grief. He and Lakshmana frantically scoured the jungle, rushing this way and that. There were times when Rama despaired. "It's all because of my stupidity! How easily I was tricked by the golden deer, and now Sita – who gave up everything for me – is in the hands of the demons!" Lakshmana comforted and sustained his brother, begging him not to give up hope. "We will find her," he insisted. "You must have hope for her sake."

On and on they travelled, asking the birds and beasts of the forest if any of them had seen Sita. They stumbled upon Jatayus, the vulture king, dying in the thicket. "Ah, Rama, Rama! I tried to stop them. A terrible, winged demon chariot bore her away. Forgive me."

"Oh, noble king," wept Rama. "There is nothing to forgive. It was my folly which brought about this disaster." He soothed the bird's feathers and tried to make him more comfortable. "Did you see which way they went?" he asked softly.

"South. They went south," whispered the bird faintly with his last dying breath. Then his soul fled from his body, and Jatayus was taken up to Vishnu's heaven in a blazing chariot of fire.

Once again, Lakshmana lifted his distraught brother and urged him not to give up hope. "Come! We must go south," he said, and led his brother on through the forest.

And so began a long search for Sita. They encountered many dangers, and fought fierce battles with beasts and demons. The birds and animals of the forest watched them caringly. They sent messages on ahead by wing and call and by fleet foot: "Where is Sita? Has anyone seen Sita?" On and on, southwards, they travelled, until one day, when the monsoon rain clouds came lumbering like grey elephants across the sky, they arrived at the mountain kingdom of Sugriva, the Ape King.

"Have you seen Sita?" Rama and Lakshmana asked the friendly apes who came bounding down the rocks to meet them.

"We saw Ravana's chariot fly overhead. It was flying towards his island kingdom of Lanka. We didn't see who was inside, but there must have been a maiden, for bracelets were thrown from the chariot, and we found them."

The apes led the two princes before Sugriva, who listened to their story. Sugriva sent for the bracelets, to see if Rama could tell if they were Sita's. Rama held the delicate ornaments in his hands, but was so blinded by tears that he could hardly say if they were hers or not.

Suddenly a huge ape, powerful as a tree and as gold

as the sun, stepped forward. It was Sugriva's general, Hanuman. This ape son of Vayu, the Wind God, was brave and swift, cunning and clever – and above all noble and good. He had magic powers to make himself big or small and to change himself into any shape. "I'll go to Lanka alone and see if Sita is there," he said to the sorrowing princes.

"If she is there," said Sugriva, "then you can count on my armies to help rescue her."

In one magical moment, Hanuman vanished like a breath of wind, and reappeared right in the very heart of King Ravana's palace. Changing himself into a black cat, he padded across the glittering crystal floors, up the gold and silver stairways, in and out of rose-scented chambers and vast pillared halls of state. But nowhere could he find Sita. So he turned himself back into a monkey, and sprang up onto the palace walls. From here he could see the gardens all around. Suddenly he noticed lights glowing among the trees of a distant grove. He leaped from the walls into the branches of a nearby tree, down onto the lawns, and bounded across the palace gardens. There, in the centre of the grove, he found her.

Sita was leaning against a tree, pale and tragic. All around her were monstrous demon guards, with grotesque heads and evil eyes. They snorted and grunted in the moonless night, lolling over their torches as they tried to keep awake and guard the princess. Hanuman hid in the branches above her head and waited. When at last the demons all slept, he dropped silently down. "Sita!" he whispered softly. She started with alarm. "I have come from Rama! Don't lose heart, he is coming to rescue you." Sita gazed at him, her face so worn with sorrow, and tears of hope fell down her cheeks. When Hanuman saw the grief and agony that had been inflicted on this lovely princess, he lost his temper. He gave an enraged roar, which woke the demons with startled shrieks, and sent them scattering in confusion. He began to grow and grow and grow, so that soon he was towering above them like the mightiest of trees. He whirled into them with arms flying and claws ripping. Like a stampeding elephant, he charged about uprooting trees and smashing down walls. Any demon that came in his path was hurled to his death. Soon the palace was in chaos. The guards came running and the demon army descended with full force. At last, when hundreds lay dead, Hanuman was overcome and hauled before Ravana. "Kill, kill, kill!" chanted the demons.

Sita wept with horror. "Oh, brave, foolish Hanuman. What have you done? What made you think that you could take on the whole demon kingdom alone? Now we are both surely doomed."

"Kill, kill, kill," screamed the demons. But Ravana said, "No! Let us send him back, disgraced and humiliated. It will show our enemies how helpless they are."

He grasped a blazing torch and held it to Hanuman's tail. The demons shrieked with glee when they saw the ape's fine, long tail burst into flames. But their malicious joy soon changed to alarm. Hanuman began to shrink. He became so small that he slipped from his bonds and sprang away. With triumphant yells, he leaped onto the palace roof with his burning tail. Soon the palace was in flames. Then he bounded all over the city, from wall to wall and roof to roof, until fires blazed from one end to the other. When he was done, Hanuman sucked his tail to put out the fire and transported himself back to Sugriva's kingdom, leaving behind pandemonium and panic.

"Sita is on the island of Lanka!" Now Sugriva put all his forces at Rama's disposal. At his call, huge bears came lumbering out of the forest with claws and teeth as sharp as knives. Apes of every colour swung down from the rocky slopes – apes of red, green, yellow, orange and blue. They came in vast waves, shouting, "Death to Ravana! Victory to Rama and Lakshmana!" They all swept down to the shore and stared across the shining sea to the island of Lanka. But how would they cross the water?

When Ravana heard how Sugriva's forces were massing on the far shore, he laughed. "They can bellow all they like, but they'll never cross the ocean!" But a demon messenger came rushing up and shouted, "They're building a bridge!" Now the demons stared anxiously across the sea. Thousands of monkeys were hurling rocks and boulders into the sea. Day and night they worked, and soon a bridge began to creep closer and closer to the island of Lanka.

A groan of concern rumbled among the demon warriors. They had heard of Prince Rama – and how he had never been defeated in battle.

Ravana angrily rallied his forces. He summoned up

all the hideous demons of the underworld to strike terror into his enemies. Then he had Sita taken into an inner chamber in the palace and placed under heavy guard.

The city watched and waited. The sounds of the bridge-building grew nearer and nearer as the rocks were hurled on top of one another. They could hear the sounds of Sugriva's armies. Voices that shouted, "Victory to Rama! Death to Ravana!" Even in her secret prison Sita heard the shouts of Rama's name and she trembled for his safety.

Soon the cries were echoing in the palace itself, as like a vast tidal wave, Rama and his forces swept across the bridge and onto the island of Lanka.

Rushing towards them came Ravana and his armies, and the two met in ferocious combat. Flaming arrows flew all over the city, spears streaked like lightning, and rocks and boulders were hurled about like thunderbolts. Both sides killed each other in thousands, and the streets ran with blood. Rama knew that the battle would only be decided when he and Ravana met face to face in single combat. He took up his mighty bow and sheath of arrows and galloped through the lashing armies. Riding towards him through the smoke of battle came Ravana.

His ten heads glowered with hatred, his twenty eyes burning like the fires of hell. Rama fired arrow after arrow at each head. But no sooner was one struck off than another grew in its place. Then Rama took up a flaming arrowtip, given to him by Brahma himself. He aimed at the very centre of Ravana's heart, and fired. There was a rending crack as Ravana's heart split in two like an axe splits a tree. His ten heads rolled in agony as the demon king crashed down in a cloud of dust. The noise of battle ceased. There was the terrible silence of defeat. Then a voice shouted, "Rama is the victor!" and with cries of "Rama, Rama, Sita, Rama!" the apes surged forward into the palace searching for Sita. They stripped room after room, swarming across the crystal floors and up the silver and gold staircases. Then at last they found her and very gently and tenderly led her to Rama.

CHAPTER FIVE
Suffering Without End

WAS THIS THE END of Sita's suffering? She walked with her heart full of love, trembling at being before her husband once more. Humbly she knelt at his feet and kissed them. What pain did it cause Rama to stand there cold and rejecting? "You have been freed, Sita," he said finally, "and I have taken revenge on your kidnapper, but I cannot take you back as my wife, for you have lived with Ravana all this time, and I have no proof that you are without blame."

Many wept as they heard these hard words and saw Sita's form shudder with pain. At last she stood up and went to Lakshmana. "If I had known that

Rama doubted my honour all this time, I should not have found the will to live. Build me a funeral pyre, Lakshmana. I would rather die than live under a cloud of suspicion."

With breaking heart, Lakshmana did as he was told. He built a huge pyre of scented sandal wood, and drenched it with ghee and sprinkled it with sweet-smelling spices.

"Light the fire, Lakshmana," said Sita in a calm voice. Lakshmana tossed a burning brand onto the pyre, and immediately huge flames sprang up with a loud crackling. Then Sita stretched out her hands and prayed loudly. "Oh, Agni! Lord of Fire! Hear my prayer. I am innocent of any unfaithful act. Be witness to my truth and virtue." Then she leaped into the flames and vanished.

A great sob broke out from all who watched. Rama collapsed with grief and lamentation. Then suddenly, as the flames leaped higher and higher, there appeared in the middle the great god Agni himself; bright, brilliant and shining, sharp-faced, three-headed Agni, who carried Sita in his arms. "Rama! Take back your wife. She is without blame or sin."

With a cry of joy, Rama leaped forward and clasped Sita in his arms. Now was the moment of reunion. Now they embraced with true love and joy, together once more.

The exile was over. Fourteen years had finally passed. Rama, Sita and Lakshmana returned to Ayodhya in splendid triumph. Rama sat on his rightful throne with Sita at his side. So was this finally an end to Sita's suffering? It was not. Rumour and gossip ran wild through the city. How could Sita have lived in Ravana's palace all that time and remained untouched? Ugly words and whispers ran like a current; Sita is going to have a baby. How can anyone be sure it is Rama's child? When these doubts reached Rama's ears, he was filled with pain once more. People asked how Rama could rule as a noble king, with a wife who had lost her virtue? Black discontent grew so strongly among his people that at last Rama knew that Sita would have to leave. He called his brother Lakshmana.

"Oh, faithful Lakshmana," he cried. "I cannot rule my kingdom as I must while Sita's name is so defamed. Take her away from Ayodhya, far, far away."

So the sorrowing Lakshmana, ever faithful, did

as he was told. He took Sita back into the jungle. They travelled a long way southwards, back to where they had once known happiness. At last he came to a hermitage. Here lived the famous sage, Valmiki. This good, saintly man took Sita into his care. Lakshmana embraced Sita for the last time, and said farewell.

In time, Sita gave birth to twin sons called Lava and Kusa. There could be no doubt that these were the sons of Rama. They looked like him and stood like him and had all his virtues.

Sixteen years went by. Rama never knew happiness. At last, burdened by guilt and despair, he decided to perform the "horse sacrifice". A horse was set free to wander at will across the land. Rama followed it wherever it went – into whatever danger or battle – into whatever strange parts. It led him through the jungles to the south. There, one day, he came across two youths. As he gazed at them it was as though he looked into a mirror – they resembled him so perfectly. "Whose children are you?" he asked with awe.

"Our mother is called Sita. We do not know who our father is," they said.

Rama felt as though his heart would burst. He

followed the boys back to the hermitage where he begged Valmiki to let him see Sita.

But Sita had borne all the sorrow she could. "I cannot see him any more," she murmured. "Never has a wife loved her husband more, or been more faithful, but it has brought me nothing but shame and sorrow. I cannot see Rama."

Valmiki pleaded with her, until at last Sita walked out of the hermitage and stood for a moment before her husband who waited at the edge of the clearing. Then she flung her arms up to heaven.

"Oh, Mother Earth!" she called. "You who gave birth to me! Spare me any more anguish and shame. Take me back to your arms, please!"

The earth opened up as gently as a flower opens in the sunlight. Rising up from the ground came the Goddess of the Earth, Sita's mother. She sat on a shining throne, and near her was another seat. Tenderly, she reached out her hand and took her daughter to her side with loving words. "Come, my sinless child, faithful and innocent wife of Rama. Come and find peace." Then the earth closed over them and Sita disappeared from the sight of the world for ever.

Rama lay on the ground calling for death to take him too. But Lord Brahma appeared and said, "Why do you grieve, Rama, Lord of All, Incarnate of Vishnu? You know that life is just a dream, a bubble of water. Why do you despair?"

But Rama, the man, did despair, and his grief never waned until he too died. Then he became Vishnu once more, and when he went up to his own heaven – there was his beloved Sita waiting for him with all the smiles of angels. She was now the goddess Lakshmi, and joyfully received her Lord.

For ever after they listened to the prayers which rose from the lips of men ... Rama, Sita, Rama ... and the world never forgot the story of Rama and Sita.

BACKGROUND NOTES
TO THE STORIES

Savitri Lord Yama is the God of Death.
He decides the life span of each human, and he
decides who goes to heaven and who goes to hell.
However, as with many Hindu stories, dialogue with
the gods is possible, even to the extent of pleading
a case for being returned to life.

This is one of the most famous stories as it
illustrates perfectly how a wife's devotion to her
husband, combined with penance and prayer,
enabled her to meet Lord Yama face to face and
bargain for Satyvan's life.

Damayanti The story of Nala and Damayanti
is contained within the great epic collection of stories,
"The Mahabharata", which has its origins at least
3000 years ago.

Nala is traditionally an incarnation of Manu,
the first man on earth and the first law-giver. He and

Damayanti are victims of the whims and rivalries of the gods and demons, but the story demonstrates how with steadfastness and loyalty humans can win through.

Sita The story of Rama and Sita was first written down by the hermit, Valmiki, in about the second century BC but had been popularly known for centuries before that. Composed in the form of an epic poem known as "The Ramayana", its length and richness of material makes it comparable with the Greek "Odyssey".

The story, however, is best known throughout the Hindu world not through being read but by being danced and enacted in towns and villages with singers and story-tellers.

Rama is traditionally an incarnation of the "Supreme Being" Vishnu, while Sita is an incarnation of the goddess Lakshmi. They both epitomize the finest qualities looked for in the perfect man and woman.

GLOSSARY

Brahma The Hindu trinity consists of Brahma, Vishnu and Shiva. Brahma is the Supreme Being, the Cause of Everything. Although he is depicted with four heads and is associated with the swan, he is really without form because he is in everything. His followers invoke him in sound, through the syllable Ôm.

Brahmans They are the highest caste, the priestly caste. They will only eat food prepared by other Brahmans. If this isn't possible, they prepare their own. In India, many Brahmans are cooks.

The Charioteer After Brahmans, the warrior caste is the next highest. It is the caste of kings. The chariot is a special symbol. The charioteer has been likened to "The Self" who holds in his hands the reins which guide the senses in the form of horses.

Cleanliness and Purity The Hindus are very strict about the habits of cleanliness and purity. Purification is absolutely vital before prayer, and praying and purification are often enacted together.

Hands and feet must be washed before prayer, and water drunk. Food may only be taken with the right hand. Toilet cleansing MUST be performed with the left hand.

Cows and Elephants All animals in India are sacred, and have a variety of connotations. The cow is perhaps the most sacred because she gives milk and the world was created, according to the Hindus, by the churning of the Ocean of Milk.

Cows need pastures to feed from, so of course the monsoon rains are vital. The Hindus use the analogy of the cows and elephants being the bringers and encompassers of rain. In the dry season the cows and elephants have been imprisoned by the Drought Demons. They wait for Lord Indra, riding on his elephant, to come and fight the Drought Demons and release the cows and elephants. These are seen in the form of the fat rain clouds which come drifting across the sky when the monsoon comes.

The Himalayas This, traditionally, is where the gods live. Indra was the Lord of Heaven and it is referred to as "Indra's Heaven", but he does not decide who lives and who dies. This is Lord Yama's job.

Incarnation This is not quite the same as reincarnation. A god chooses to continue his existence in an animal or human. So he occupies that body which becomes an incarnation of him, such as Vishnu, Krishna, Rama.

Lotus The lotus is considered the most perfect of flowers. It floats on water. Its petals unfold and the shape of the petals are likened to the shape of eyes. The goddess Lakshmi emerged out of the Ocean of Milk during the creation of the world seated on a lotus. The pale creamy pink and white colour of the flower gives it a radiancy which invites comparison with beautiful people, men or women.

Manu Manu was, traditionally, the first man on earth. He was a "mind born" son of Brahma, born from his thoughts. He is a holy man with special godlike powers, a rishi. He became the "Law Giver". He also built an ark and saved living things from the flood. Nala was supposed to be an incarnation of Manu.

Marriage Once a girl is married she becomes the property of her husband and there is no obligation on the part of her family to have any further contact with her.

Monkeys The monkeys are particularly sacred in India because of the help they gave Rama in crossing the sea to Lanka. Lanka is the island of Ceylon, now known as Sri Lanka.

Rama Rama is an incarnation of Vishnu, the god Preserver.

Reincarnation It is believed all living things are born and reborn in a never-ending cycle. There is a recognized scale of rebirth of higher and lower levels. Someone who has lead a good life can expect to be reborn (reincarnated) into a higher and better life form, human or animal. A bad life gets you reincarnated down the scale. The final goal is to get to heaven, Nirvana, where reincarnation ceases.

Sita Sita is an incarnation of Lakshmi, Goddess of Love and Good Fortune.

Swan The swan is traditionally Brahma's "vehicle". All the main gods have their own animal vehicles: Indra rides on an elephant, Brahma on a swan, Lord Yama on a buffalo, Lord Shiva on a bull and Vishnu on a serpent.

Swayamvara This is the ceremony when a princess chooses her husband by garlanding him.

Vishnu Vishnu is one of the Hindu Trinity of Brahma, the Creator; Vishnu, the Preserver; and Shiva, the Destroyer. He became the most popular god and is incarnated in two of the most worshipped of gods, Krishna and Rama.

Yama Yama is the Lord of the Dead. Hindus believe that their life span is already ordained. However, they also believe that in exceptional circumstances it is possible to appeal to Lord Yama to extend life or to give it back.

JAMILA GAVIN was born in India and moved to the UK as a teenager. She studied music, then worked for the BBC before becoming a full-time writer of stories and plays for children. She is now one of Britain's most acclaimed children's authors, winning the Whitbread Award and being shortlisted for the Carnegie Medal for her novel *Coram Boy*, which was later staged at the National Theatre. Jamila lives in Gloucestershire.